ON THE EDGE OF FOREVER

WITH THE BAND
BOOK THREE

TANYA RENEE

Serenade Publishing

Serenade Publishing

www.serenadepublishing.com

For those that struggle to reconcile their mistakes and need a little grace. This novel is for you.

ALSO BY TANYA RENEE

Primrose Series

Prairie Sky

Prairie Nights

Prairie Fire

Prairie Hearts

Prairie Sound

Prairie Rain

Prairie Prestige

Prairie Roads

With The Band

Finding Direction

Love Notes

On The Edge Of Forever

PROLOGUE

*I*t was getting late; the clock read past midnight and Rex hadn't seen Harlow for an hour at least. The music was loud, booming from portable speakers somewhere in the two-story house. Some lame boy band shit that made Rex cringe. Students danced in the living room, and others milled on the sides of the makeshift dance floor, drinking stale kegger beer from red solo cups. These dull high school parties were no longer his scene, and the urge to ditch his girlfriend and head to the bar to check out the Friday night eye candy was beyond tempting.

It's not that there weren't pretty girls at this party. Of course, the St. Augustine Regional School cuties were out in full force tonight with their short skirts, crop tops and tight skinny jeans. In fact, from where he was standing, leaning against the kitchen island, sipping on a flat beer and surveying the living room, he spotted at least five girls he would love to deflower if given the opportunity. *That is if I weren't with Harlow.* His internal voice of reason tried to remind him, as he downed the rest of his beer in an attempt to strangle any guilt he might feel from his wandering thoughts.

A flash of blonde hair across the room broke him from his dirty musings, but when the blonde head turned around, it wasn't Harlow. *Where the hell is she?* Rex shook his head and turned back to the keg, pouring more of the putrid liquid into his cup with impatience. Last time he saw her, one of her friends pulled her away, talking about some girly shit like grad dresses or something. *Fuck, I'm bored.*

"Hey, Rex." a sultry voice sounded beside him, as a warm roaming hand grazed down his shoulder and rested on his arm. Glancing down, he saw long, pristinely painted red fingernails, gripped his forearm tightly.

He turned, knowing exactly who it was, his lips curling up into a fiendish grin. "Well, if it isn't Tess Simpson," he drawled, taking in the tall, leggy brunette from his graduating class. "How the hell are you?"

"Good," she replied, drawing dangerously closer, caressing her long fingers languidly up and down his bicep. "Even better now, seeing you here."

Rex threw his head back in a laugh, his voice deep and husky, knowing what an unrepentant flirt Tess was, and how she had a reputation for taking what she wanted when she wanted it. Despite this knowledge, he made no move to step away from her, letting her hand go from caressing his arm to resting on his stomach as she curled herself around him, her hot breath on his neck. This was the most interesting thing to happen at this party, and although he knew it was wrong to be seen with her here in public, in this moment he was here for it.

"Where's your little Tinkerbell?" she asked, glancing around and feigning a smile.

"No idea," he replied with a shrug as he drew the solo cup to his lips, took a sip of the piss-warm beer and winced.

"Well, her loss is my gain." Tess cooed, leaning in, her lips brushing his ear. She smelled like hops and sin, and surely, he was going to hell for letting her get this close. "This party is super lame, and I saw someone head upstairs with some pot. Do you want to help me find them?" She asked, her voice low and sinful.

Rex had smoked pot before and had to admit he enjoyed the high. Of course, the first time he smoked it was with Harlow, and that night ended in a very passionate quickie in the stall of a public bathroom at their favorite diner. The thought of that made his groin tighten painfully and goosebumps rise on his skin. *Fuck this party sucks!* He turned to Tess and replied, "Yeah, I could use a high right now."

Her meticulously painted red lips curled up in a wicked grin, and she looped her arm through his as they exited the kitchen, heading towards the staircase. Climbing the stairs, the euphoric smell of pot assaulted Rex's nose, and he breathed deeply, inhaling the sweet smell. They followed the haze of smoke to a second-floor family room where five students, three guys and two girls sat, passing around a joint. Rex grinned, thinking about how much better this party was about to be once he was buzzed. Slugging back the last of his warm beer, he set the cup on a table beside the couch as he brazenly plucked the joint from the fingers of a well-known stoner and took a long deep drag, passing it over to Tess and watching her do the same. She passed the joint over to another kid, and they watched as it was passed around, making it's way back to them. They both took another hit. With hazy eyes, Tess stumbled on her high heels into Rex's arms, his eyes zoning in on her red lips, far too inviting not to want to kiss. Fuck, *she's hot.* Steadying her, they both laughed as she grabbed his hand, leading him out of the family room and down the hallway into a bedroom at the end. As soon as she dragged him inside, Tess closed the door and flashed him a devilish grin as she rested her back on the closed door.

"Now that I have you all to myself." She purred. "I think we could be wickedly naughty together, don't you think?." she asked, slowly bunching her skirt up to reveal very tiny black lace panties, as her mouth parted, and the tip of her tongue moistened her lips.

Rex's eyes immediately followed her tongue, licking his own lips in response, his libido kicking in and his body hardening instantly. His jeans tight and pressing against the zipper of his fly, he watched as Tess hooked her fingers into the sides of her panties and slid them down, leaving her bare before him. Crooking a finger his way to beckon him over, the look on her face was one of a woman about to get exactly what she wanted. His thoughts no longer his own, all blood having rushed south, he complied like a lapdog, crowding her against the door as she reached down and popped the button of his jeans, slowly working the zipper down. Damn, *I want to touch her. To fuck her. Just once. No one needs to know* were his last thoughts as he took what he wanted from her, with no consideration as to consequence or loyalty.

15 minutes later, he stumbled out of the bedroom high on lust and drugs. Hair disheveled, red lipstick smeared on his mouth, Tess giggling and hanging on his arm as he turned and was met by Harlow standing in the hallway, two friends at her side and absolute devastation and disgust in her beautiful ocean blue eyes.

CHAPTER 1

*L*iving your life in a constant state of regret wasn't really living, was it? And yet, that's where Rex Johnson found himself. As a drummer for a popular indie rock band, he had taken the sex, drugs and rock n roll thing quite seriously. At the age of 30 Rex had bedded more women than he could count, had drunk himself stupid at least as many times, and had somehow with only the idiocy he could manage, got himself caught deep in the drug scene of St. Augustine, almost getting himself killed in the process. Now two years into his sobriety, scarred both externally and internally, he had finally moved out of his parent's home and was living on his own again. Even though he had more freedom, he still felt like a prisoner. A prisoner of his relentless self-deprecating thoughts and deepest regrets.

Growing up in St. Augustine, he loved this small city and grew up in a traditional home, with two loving parents and two younger sisters. He could never remember a time of needing anything. His parents, the owners of a large trucking company, had made a good living for themselves and gave their three children everything they could need and more. He had a wonderful childhood with more than his share of opportunities.

Rex had two younger sisters who were smart, educated, and ambitious. He adored them and did the protective big brother thing whenever a guy came sniffing around them. Never would he let any man treat his sisters the way he had treated women in the past. Like tissues you throw away after one use. Looking back, he wasn't proud of his promiscuous ways and knew he had broken more than a few hearts along the way. Using his blue mohawk and badass rocker persona to lure women in with his sexy Rexy ways. *Sexy Rexy, my nickname and alter ego. Fuck, I hate it now.* That nickname represented the man he was before he was beaten within an inch of his life, and just the thought of that time made him sick. He was a womanizer back then, plain and simple, and over the years he had never emotionally attached himself to any woman. Just taking and never giving. *That is of course all but one.* Still to this day, the only heart he broke that ever mattered to him was Harlow Ford's.

Having met the blue-eyed beauty at 16, he was instantly captivated by the 15-year-old freshman. Harlow had long blonde hair the color of golden wheat in the sunshine, ocean blue eyes, a tight petite body, and adorable pouty pink lips, that he knew he wanted to kiss as soon as he met her. She was light, effervescent, and confident beyond her years. And Harlow was infatuated with him from day one.

They started out as most kids their age did, going out

on dates, hanging out with friends, and spending time together between classes and on weekends. A few months into dating, it was on one of those weekends that they found themselves on his dingy basement couch with his parents and sisters upstairs, movie credits rolling on the TV and them losing their virginities in what could only be described as a stereotypical awkward teenage fashion.

From that day, he lusted after her like only a horny teenager could, and she ate up every bit of affection he offered her. Thinking back, the three years they dated were wild, fun and fiery. A mixture of hormones, self-discovery and clashes of opinion that always ended in a passionate makeout session followed by fumbling, raw, dirty sex in precarious places. In the last year they were together, after Rex graduated high school and as Harlow was in her senior year figuring out her future, they fought more than they didn't. That was the year Rex stopped caring what anyone thought, and the year Harlow had finally had enough.

Rex would never forget the day they broke up, and still to this day he was ashamed of how it all went down. He had done her dirty, cheated, got caught and deserved all the anger and hurt she threw back at him. Sometimes when he closed his eyes, he could still see her beautiful face red with anger, her voice cracking with her betrayed words, her quivering chin and the fire and tears in her beautiful blue eyes. That image had haunted more than a few of his dreams.

* * *

REX LOOKED AT HIS WATCH; it was almost time for his sobriety meeting. His sponsor, Jeremy, sent him the address, and he had to do a double take as he stared up at the sign on the trendy coffee shop that read, Meeting Grounds. *Clever.* Entering the building, Rex looked around, taking in the ultra cool relaxed décor and instantly felt at ease. With its dark, swanky leather couches and chairs, making up small seating areas, square dark wood tables with black accents and black chairs, the space simply invited one to come in, sip their favorite coffee and read a book. Along one wall was floor-to-ceiling brickwork with black industrial-looking sconces adding light, and in the middle was a long dark wood coffee bar. The building was narrow and split into two distinct spaces. The front of the building was a coffee shop, and the back a meeting space with more couches and chairs for lounging or, in his case, for his sobriety meeting. A trendy sliding barn door separated the two spaces. Rex approached the coffee bar to be met by a pretty brunette in her late teens, and she offered him a sweet, friendly smile.

"Can I help you?" She asked in a bubbly tone.

Rex couldn't help but grin back at the effervescent teen. "Yes, can I have a large coffee, black, please?"

"Coming right up!" she exclaimed happily as she grabbed a takeout cup and filled it with the black liquid. She popped a lid on top and turned to hand him his coffee.

"I got it." A voice sounded behind him, and he turned to be met with his sponsor Jeremy's smiling face and him holding out a $10 bill. "Can I get the same, please?" he asked the girl, and she nodded, turning to fix him a cup as well.

Jeremy Zarensky, in his mid 50s was tall, had an athletic build and had hair the color of polished silverware. He had brown eyes and a big, bright smile that was incredibly contagious. Every time Rex looked at him, it was hard for him to imagine that he too was once a drug addict and had struggled with sobriety for nearly three decades.

Jeremy turned to Rex and clapped him on the back in greeting. "Hey there, Rex. Are you ready for this next phase?"

Rex took a sip of his coffee and nodded as he replied with a big exhale, "Yeah, I think so."

Jeremy paid for the coffees and led Rex towards the back of the coffee shop, where several other people had already gathered. "This next phase with SMART Recovery will help you immensely. I know myself that what I learned at these meetings has been invaluable to me in managing my addiction and bringing back a sense of normalcy to my life."

Rex nodded, and as much as he wished he was done attending meetings, he had made a commitment to his family and to his band that he would do everything he could to stay sober. This was his last phase to complete, so for the next year these SMART Recovery meetings were going to be part of his commitment towards sobriety in the long term.

"Holly, I'm so sorry, I'm late!" a voice exclaimed behind them, making Rex instinctively turn to see a shock of golden blonde hair behind the coffee bar.

Rex slowed his steps, his brows furrowed, the voice so incredibly familiar to him as he followed Jeremy into the back room. He took a seat next to Jeremy as the rest of the group gathered, but he found his eyes roaming to the front of the coffee shop, watching a petite blonde woman dressed in all black wipe tables near the front of the shop. She looked so familiar, but it was hard to make out her features from this distance. A middle-aged woman entered the back room and smiled at everyone as she slid the barn door closed, forcing Rex's attention back to the group. The woman took a seat, a clipboard in her hand, and smiled as she began his final phase of recovery.

90 MINUTES LATER, they emerged, Rex feeling lighter, like the heavy weight he continued to carry was starting to lift off his chest. With just one meeting, he felt like he might someday have an independent life, free from his addiction. He had thought about what that would look like so many times. Having been the sex, drugs and rock n roll cliché so long he didn't know who he was without it, but now two years sober, two years celibate and two years alone he could finally think about what it may be like to be in a relationship and God willing find what his bandmates had found. All of whom were happily married, with the women of their dreams and growing or starting families. Whenever he spent time with his pseudo-family, he felt those pangs of yearning for what they had. The love of one incredible woman and children to carry on his name.

"We'll see you next week, same time, same place."

Jeremy said as he walked towards the door. "Message me if you need me, okay?"

"I will." Rex replied as he slowed at the coffee bar. He turned to the same teen that was there before and put down his takeout cup. "Could I get another cup? Really great coffee, by the way."

"Thanks! The owner of this place is all about quality and only gets the best beans." She said with a smile as she poured him another cup. "Did you want anything to eat? We have these amazing cookies from a bakery in Primrose."

Rex's eyes brightened and replied, "My bandmate's sister owns that place. Everything you Knead?"

"Yeah, that's the one! They are so good!" she exclaimed, rolling her eyes back. "Can I get you one?" she asked, showing him a batch of giant chocolate chip cookies under a glass dome. He had eaten his share of those cookies over the years, and he knew how decadent they were.

"Yeah, I'll have one." he replied with a smile.

She plated him a cookie as he handed her a bill, telling her to keep the change. Turning, he spotted the long green leather couch looking like as good a place as any to take a seat. Getting comfortable on the couch, he pulled out his phone and reached for his cookie, taking a big bite and setting it back down on the plate. He shook his head in appreciation, the decadent chocolate, sugar and butter melding in his mouth into a perfect bite. *Marnie should win the Academy Award for baking*. He chewed and swiped open his phone, scrolling through several messages. Rami about band practice tomorrow. His mom asking if he wanted to come over for Dinner Sunday night, and Steve asked how his meeting went. Mindlessly, he reached down for his cookie and paused, not feeling it there. Glancing down at the plate, he saw it was empty, with just a few crumbs left as evidence that it had indeed been there. Rex's eyes darted around and fixed on the cutest blonde, blue-eyed boy of around 4 or 5 years old with chocolate smeared on his lips, half the cookie in his hand and a mischievous twinkle in his eye. Rex couldn't help but laugh at the adorable cookie thief, offered him a tender smile and asked, "Do you like cookies?"

The little boy nodded, taking another big bite, and Rex chuckled as he heard a commotion coming from the back of the coffee shop.

"Tyson!" a familiar voice sounded as it got closer. "I told you to stay in my office until I was done checking the stock."

Rex turned to the source of the voice. The blonde woman he saw earlier was making her way over to the little boy, and he had to do a double take. Before him, dressed all in black, her blonde hair a little shorter than he remembered, but with the same ocean blue eyes and once memorized gorgeous pouty lips, was none other than Harlow Ford.

Harlow, not paying any mind to him, rushed over to the little boy and scrutinized him, her hands on her hips. "Where did you get the cookie?"

"He stole it from my plate." Rex answered as she slowly turned to face him, and her eyes widened, registering who she was talking to. She took a step back, putting her hand over her heart, complete shock on her face as their eyes locked. *She still has the most beautiful eyes.*

Harlow broke their stare. Her brows furrowed for a moment. She cleared her throat, and she shook her head, glancing at the little boy and then back to Rex as she asked with disbelief in her tone, "Rex?"

"Hi," he said simply, not believing she was there in front of him too. He glanced down at the little boy, now realizing he was the spitting image of Harlow. "Is this little fella yours?"

She let out a little giggle, the sound as amazing as he remembered, and she rounded the couch picking up the little boy and taking a seat on the other end of the couch settling the boy on her lap as she offered him a reluctant smile, "Yes, this is my son Ty, or Tyson...wow, Rex Johnson, it's been forever ago."

Rex smiled down at the little boy, and his eyes trailed back up to Harlow's. "It has been at least 12 years." He replied as he glanced down at the little boy again, and his head filled with a million questions. He glanced down at her left hand, no wedding ring, but curiosity overtook his mouth before he could stop the question. "Are you married?"

Harlow let out a breath she seemed to have been holding, her face turning ashen, and wrapped her arms around her son, pulling him into her protectively as she answered, "I was."

Rex scanned her expression, immediately knowing he shouldn't pry, and he nodded as he met her gaze and took her in fully. She looked exactly the same, as if no time had passed. Still so impossibly beautiful. "You look the same. I mean different but the same."

She touched her hair, and instantly he wanted to reach out and touch it too. She always had the most incredibly soft hair that he loved to run his fingers through. "I guess I should take the compliment." She said with a hesitant smile and a giggle. "Mostly I'm a harried divorced mom with coffee spilled on my shirt."

She's divorced. Rex stowed that information away as he smiled, feeling more buoyant at the sight of her and this conversation than he had in years.

* * *

HARLOW STARED into the blue eyes of her once high school sweetheart and started chiding herself internally at how much she missed his intense gaze.

"Now, you look completely different." She said, squinting her eyes and perusing him carefully as she asked, "Ditched the blue mohawk?" Offering her a reluctant smile, he reached for his coffee and took a sip before he answered, her question seeming to have struck a nerve. "I mean, you look different, but good. You look healthy..." she started, looking down at Tyson's blonde locks and smoothing them nervously with her hand. "...I mean, I... read what happened to you, and you look like you're in a better place."

Rex's face fell a little with her observation, and immediately she regretted bringing it up in conversation. It couldn't have been easy being in the spotlight and having your personal battles splashed around media like fodder for gossip.

"Yeah, I'm in a better place." He replied. "Two years sober and just had my first SMART Recovery meeting," he said, gesturing towards the back of the coffee shop.

Harlow's heart warmed at the thought of him being part of that meeting. That was exactly why she had opened this coffee shop. She wanted it to be a safe place for everyone, and working with the local chapter of the Addictions Foundation, she made the back of her coffee shop a meeting place to get the guidance and help they needed.

"That was my vision for this place when I opened it a few months ago. I wanted this to be a place for people to meet, whether it be for coffee or more."

"So, this is your place?" he asked, his eyes darting around the space and his smile growing wide. "I really like it. I feel like I could curl up on this couch with a book and spend the whole day here," he added, running his hand over the back of the green leather.

"That's exactly what I wanted with this place." She said. "It's supposed to be a safe and relaxing place to just "be" for a while."

"I think you accomplished that," he replied, meeting her gaze and then letting his eyes drift down to the little boy in her arms. Rex leaned in, his eyes sparkling as he put out his fist to Tyson for him to bump. "Hi Tyson, I'm Rex."

The little boy gave him a chocolate smile and bumped his little fist to Rex's. "Like a T-Rex?" he asked in a sweet, soft voice. "I like dinosaurs."

Rex let out a boisterous laugh. "If you want to call me T-Rex, go right ahead, little buddy. I believe we're friends now that we've shared that cookie."

Tyson smiled as Holly walked by with empty mugs in her hands, and she glanced at Ty, letting out a little giggle. "Harlow, I can take Ty in the back and get him cleaned up if you want to visit some more." She offered, glancing between her and Rex.

Harlow liked Holly Willst as soon as she met her. The girl reminded her so much of herself at that age, before life took over and things got complicated. She was sweet, funny and full of life, and the customers loved her.

"Yes, thank you," Harlow replied, lifting Ty off her lap and setting him down on his feet. "You go with Holly, and she'll help you get cleaned up."

"C'mon Ty. Let's get that chocolate off your face," Holly said as she gave Harlow a quick wink and nodded towards Rex. It was subtle, but she saw it. Harlow watched them go before her eyes returned to Rex's. *Man, he looks good.* Sans mohawk, with medium brown hair cut short, almost shaven, his square jaw matured into an edgy masculine profile and those mesmerizing blue eyes. She hadn't realized how much she missed his handsome face. Despite their brutal breakup, she had kept track of him over the years and had even seen him in concert several times, choosing to watch him from the back rather than front and centre. As bad as the end of their relationship was, she still appreciated her time with him and all the things they experienced together. He was her first for pretty much everything, and their time together was a huge part of her history that she couldn't ignore. Besides, she had been there at the beginning of Prairie Sound, and seeing the guys she used to hang out with hit it big was thrilling.

"I've followed your career over the years." She confessed, resting her hands in her lap and curling her legs up into a criss-cross position on the couch. "It's amazing what you guys have accomplished."

Rex let out a long exhale as he replied. "It's been a ride."

She smiled, the doorbell chiming as a large group of twenty somethings entered and hesitantly; she got to her feet. "I've got to help these customers, but I'll get you another cookie."

Rex laughed, "Don't bother. I need to get going anyway," he said, rising from the couch, his takeout cup in hand.

Her lips curled up into a smile as she took in all of him and found herself inadvertently biting the corner of her lip as she used to do when he was in the room. *He really does look fantastic.* "I'll see you next week then."

As she walked towards the counter, she could feel his intense blue eyes watching her go, and even though her head and heart told her not to, Harlow had to admit she liked it.

CHAPTER 2

Rex jumped up in bed, his body drenched with sweat and his mind locked on the nightmare he had just had. It started like all his nightmares did, getting surrounded by five guys, all of them closing in on him as one landed a punch to his stomach. He could almost feel the seething pain in his bones as they continued to punch, kick and stomp on him. This time though, rather than seeing the light fade to black as it always did, he saw a flash of golden hair keeping him lucid. He shook his head, images wanting to take shape in his mind again. Rex hated this, the post-traumatic stress of getting beaten nearly to death still haunting him. Yet, somehow seeing that golden hair kept him clearheaded, gave him a reason to not drift into unconsciousness again. He ran his hand over his head, now cut short almost to his scalp, and hung his head in his hands as he tried to calm his rapidly beating heart.

Swinging his legs out of bed, he padded out of his room and into the ensuite to grab a towel to wipe the sweat from his body. Dabbing his body, he walked into the open space of his living room/kitchen and opened the refrigerator. Reaching in, he grabbed a bottle of Coca Cola and twisted the cap off. He tossed the cap onto the counter as he took a long, deep swig of the cola, letting the sugary sweetness soothe his shaken nerves. Glancing at the cola in his hand, he let out a little chuckle and shook his head. *One vice for another.*

Rex glanced over at his phone charging in its docking station and reached for it. Swiping it open, he entered his Facebook app and typed Harlow Ford into the search engine. Instantly there she was, in all her gorgeous blonde, blue-eyed glory. *Why have I never looked her up? Because the last time you saw her, she was walking out of your life, hurt and angry and telling you she never wanted to see you again,* his voice of reason answered. Shaking his head, he couldn't believe what a cocky asshole he was back then. No regard for her and her feelings, complete selfishness, his regular MO. Finding her photos, he scrolled through them, finding albums of her son Tyson. He stopped, taking in a photo of her, a newborn in her arms and next to her a handsome blonde man with blue eyes too. *This must be her ex-husband.* The man's arm was around her, and she was nestled into his side, the sleeping baby in her arms. *A beautiful family.* He continued to scroll, photo after photo of Tyson, from infant to now. So many photos of Harlow, laughing, smiling, playing with her son and his father not in a single one. *I wonder if he isn't part of Tyson's life.* A complex feeling of relief for himself and sadness for them washed over him with his observance. Every little boy deserved to have his father be present, and yet he couldn't help but feel hopeful knowing Harlow was single. *You don't even have the right to think of her that way. You betrayed her and shattered her heart.* Yet as Rex sat back on his couch, scrolling pictures and getting a glimpse into Harlow's life, part of him wished he could be a part of it.

* * *

HARLOW STARTLED AWAKE, hearing Tyson cry out in his sleep as she sat there listening and waiting to see if he would settle. With silence falling on their apartment, she laid her head back down on her pillow, but her eyes refused to close. She stared into the darkness, vaguely making out the ceiling above her. Thoughts kept running through her head, and she tried to close her eyes to no avail. She glanced over at her phone and reached for it, swiping open the screen. Entering her Google search, she typed in Rex Johnson, drummer for Prairie Sound. Hundreds of pictures and articles popped up. Headlines about the bad boy of Prairie Sound getting beaten, head-lines about his drug use and time in rehab. Candid pictures popped up, selfies of him with women, many of whom were scantily clad, kissing his cheeks and their hands on his body. *He certainly did live the rocker life,* she thought as she scrolled through the pictures. *Did.* The word hung in the air like a question mark. Rex seemed different when she saw him, like a better version of himself. Not the same person she walked away from, betrayed and angry, all those years ago.

She closed her eyes, letting her hand fall to the mattress, still holding her phone. Having carried a deep animosity towards Rex and how he treated her at the end of their relationship, his betrayal haunted her for the rest of her teens and into her twenties. She seldom dated, not trusting men as a result, until she met Brendon. Brendon was impossibly handsome, sweet, funny, and he made her laugh. He was from an affluent family, and instantly they liked her, welcoming her into their brood. Brendon was like a knight in shining armour to her, healing her heart, and very quickly she had fallen in love with him. It wasn't until they had been dating a year that she started to see cracks in his armour. It started out small, the odd late night, knocking on her apartment door, red-eyed and fidgety. Not his usual cool, calm demeanour. This carried on for another year until they got engaged and she found him passed out on the bathroom floor of the engagement party venue, white powder under his nose. She begged him to stop using, talked to his parents, and they had an intervention, sending him to rehab.

Brendon returned, the same man she first met, and they were married and excited to start their lives together. Five short months after their wedding, Harlow found out she was pregnant, and that's when things took a turn again. Countless nights she spent awake, their child growing in her belly and her husband out, with no idea where he had gone. Of course, every time he came back, he apologized, would shower her with affection and tell her what she wanted to desperately hear. Tyson was born, and for a long time everything seemed normal. Brendon made a conscious effort to spend time at home, and their relationship was on solid ground. When her mother invited her for a day of pampering for her 25th birthday,

Brendon insisted she go and that he was excited to spend the day with their 6-month-old son. When she returned later that night, Brendon was passed out on the couch, with a line of cocaine on their glass coffee table and their son beside him in a playpen, red-faced and crying, his diaper soiled through his clothes and into the mattress. That was the night she packed up whatever she could carry and left him.

She shook her head, the memory of that night too much to bear. Sitting up, she turned, setting her feet down on the cold hardwood floor and held her head in her hands. Every time she thought of that night, she could hear Ty's screaming, see his red wet face, and smell the stench from his soiled clothes and diaper. *What if Ty got a hold of the drugs Brendon was snorting? Was this the first time he had gotten high with their son in the room?* These questions were still unanswered to this day.

Hot, stinging tears pricked Harlow's eyes, and she squeezed them shut, willing them to stop as she thought of her late husband. After she left him and filed for divorce, he was found only a few short months later overdosed in his car, in the parking lot of their apartment. having snorted cocaine laced with Fentanyl. An involuntary tear rolled down her cheek, and she quickly swiped it away with the heel of her hand. It had been four years since he had passed, and it still haunted her. When she found out what had happened, she went through a phase of feeling responsible for his demise. Maybe she should have stayed, stood beside him and insisted he get help. She could have gotten his family involved again, and if she had done a better job to seek out support, maybe he would still be here, sober and part of their son's life. Years later, she knew that thought wasn't healthy as she had done the best she could at the time to protect their young son. Perhaps that was why she opened Meeting Grounds and offered the Addictions Foundation her back room for meetings. She wanted to make up for what she hadn't done and didn't know when Brendon was alive.

Picking up her phone again, she swiped it open and scrolled past new stories about Prairie Sound and Rex finding a link to his Facebook Profile. She clicked on it to be met with his smiling face and gorgeous blue eyes. It was the new Rex, not the old blue mohawked bad boy, and she liked how he looked. Rex was always so handsome, with his masculine jawline and blue eyes a rich indigo color. Now without the distracting mohawk, she could see the man behind the persona, raw and revealed, and it made her heart flutter just like it used to when she looked at him. *You don't know him now, Harlow. Be careful.* Her inner voice warned as she looked into his eyes and knew instantly she wasn't going to listen.

WALKING into the studio at Casa Perez, Rex was met by Rami holding his 9-month-old son, Micah, sleeping soundly on his shoulder. Little Micah's cheeks were red, and you could see the sweat glistening on his soft skin. Rex approached quietly, offering Rami a smile and placing a gentle hand on the baby's damp with sweat head.

Rami turned his chair to face Rex and returned his smile as he said, "He's teething, and Savanah has gotten so little sleep lately. No one knows yet, but she is expecting again and is so exhausted."

"Congrats, man. Wow, you waste no time." Rex whispered with a waggle of his eyebrows.

Rami smirked. "Not planned, but it's early, so we're still keeping things on the down low for now." Rami glanced at the clock on the wall. "You're early?"

Rex let out a quiet laugh, acknowledging his reputation for always being late. "Yeah, it only took me until the age of 30 to become a responsible adult."

Rami chuckled too, his shoulders shaking as he rose from his chair and settled Micah into a playpen set up in the corner. Rex looked at the sleeping baby, his heart swelling as he took in his chubby cheeks and sweet peaceful face. *Man, I want one of those.* His affection for all the kids of Prairie Sound as their beloved Uncle Rex, making him realize that fatherhood was something he desperately desired.

Rami watched him look at his son with deep affection as he asked, "You want to be a father, don't you?"

"Am I that obvious?" he asked with a longing in his voice and let out a big sigh. "I need to find the right woman first, though."

"You will. You're in a good place right now, and I know she's out there for you. You just need to be patient." Rami replied, clapping him on the shoulder.

Rex took in his words, hoping he could manifest them and have the same type of confidence that Rami had in him. The truth was, he had no confidence at all right now. Going out there and dating had lost its lustre, and the thought of meeting a woman and having to reveal his past addiction and sobriety was something he dreaded. *Would they see me as a project? Something to fix, or would they run for the door at breakneck speed?* Both were equally cringy to think of. Regardless, if he was going to date anyone, there needed to be a long game to consider, and he wouldn't date just to date. He was ready to find his forever, and he wasn't going to settle for less. Harlow's beautiful face came to the front of his mind with that thought as he shared, "I had a bit of a blast from the past happen to me the other day." he said, glancing at Rami. "I ran into Harlow Ford."

Rami leaned forward, meeting his gaze as a smile curled up his lips. "Harlow Ford. Wow, that is a blast from the past." Rami agreed as he leaned back in his chair and added, "I always liked Harlow, and moreover I liked her with you. I was always curious about what happened between you two? Other than being young and probably too reckless for your own good."

Rex ran his hand over his brush cut and sighed, leaning back against the wall. "I cheated on her, and she caught me," he confessed, shaking his head.

"Well, that would do it." Rami replied, letting out a long breath. "You never told me that."

"I wasn't exactly proud of it." Rex replied. "I have regretted it ever since. She was so good to me back then, and I was just a fuc..." he glanced down at Micah and corrected himself. "I was an idiot."

"How did Harlow react when she saw you?" Rami asked curiously.

"She was friendly, sweet, the same girl I knew back

then, but now she seems like she has been through some-thing. Like life hasn't been kind," he replied.

"What makes you say that?" Rami asked, his brows furrowing.

"She's divorced, has a young son; I don't know the entire story, but she's raising her son on her own." Rex replied.

"How old is her kid?" Rami asked, wanting to know more.

"4 maybe 5," Rex replied, a smile curling up his lips. "He looks exactly like her, blonde, blue eyes, seriously adorable kid."

Rami met his gaze as he asked, "Are you going to see her again? Did you exchange numbers?"

Rex shook his head in answer, but replied, "No numbers exchanged, but I'll see her at her coffee shop. It's this new place in St. Augustine called Meeting Grounds. It's where my SMART Recovery meetings are held. The back of the building is like a meeting place, while the front is for anyone to sit and enjoy a cup of joe."

"That sounds cool." Rami replied, putting his hands around the back of his head, and leaning back on his chair. "I have no idea what's cool and happening anymore. It would be so nice to just go for a cup of coffee without taking half the house with us," he added, glancing down at his sleeping son.

Rex let out a laugh and gave him an empathetic look. "And you're about to have two under the age of two."

Rami laughed and shook his head as he deadpanned, "Damn, hot wife." With his words, Savanah manifested at the door, and Rami's face lit up as Savanah entered the studio, her blue eyes dancing and her signature pink hair pulled up into a messy bun on top of her head. She was dressed in a hot pink sports bra top and short leggings, looking more like a Barbie doll than a 30-year-old soon to be mother of two.

"Hey there, hot mama." Rex said, taking her in and giving her a flirtatious wink.

Savanah let out a laugh. "Literally," she replied, dabbing her head with the back of her hand as she took a seat on Rami's lap, leaned in and kissed him sweetly. Rami's hand instinctively curled around hers and rested on her stomach where you could see the faintest swell of a baby bump.

"Congratulations," Rex said. "Rami just told me."

Savanah turned to Rami, giving him a chiding look. "You just couldn't keep it a secret, could you?" Rami laughed and kissed her shoulder, giving her his sexy smolder in apology and making her roll her eyes. Savanah's eyes lovingly drifted over to her sleeping son in the playpen and over to Rex as she added, "Just 11 weeks along so we haven't told anyone yet."

Rex looked at his two friends, so in love, their family growing quickly, and he took in their exhausted faces.

"You know I could babysit Micah tonight if you want to go out to dinner or a movie," he offered, glancing down at the sweet sleeping baby in the playpen. "Last time I babysat, Micah had fun with Uncle Rex. Plus, it's supposed to be a nice night. Perhaps we'll go for a walk, get some fresh air and he'll sleep well for you tonight."

"Are you sure?" Rami asked, hopefulness in his eyes.

"100%."

Savanah got up from Rami's lap and walked over to Rex, leaning down and planting a big kiss on his cheek. "You, Rex Johnson, are a saint."

Rex laughed and gave her a nod as she lifted a sleeping Micah from the playpen, cuddled him close to her chest and slipped past him as she mouthed, *thank you.*

* * *

"ALRIGHT THERE, MICAH," Rex said, sliding the baby boy into his stroller and crouching down he tucked a blanket around his legs and reached for a spit up cloth, wiping the drool from his chin. Micah gave him a gummy grin, just a few little chicklet teeth in his mouth, and making Rex chuckle as he said, "You smile like that at the ladies, and you'll have them all chasing after you."

Grabbing the diaper bag, he tucked it into the bottom of the stroller and made his way down the driveway towards the sidewalk leading to downtown Primrose. The day had been hot, a sweltering late May Day but now with it being early evening the hottest part of the day was behind them, and a refreshing breeze made its presence known with the rustle of new leaves on the budding trees. They walked past the school, passing the feed mill, Micah pointing his chubby little finger at the big feed truck parked in front and speaking his baby gibberish. They passed the hardware store and Isley Construction, the sign for Everything You Knead coming into view, just down the sidewalk.

"Let's go say hi to Aunt Marnie," he said to Micah as they got to the entrance of the bakery. An older woman exited the bakery, offered them a kind smile, and held the door open for them as he rolled in.

"Rex!" Marnie exclaimed as she rounded the counter and took him in with the stroller and her nephew. "And Micah! Babysitting, I see."

Rex gave her a hug as Marnie unstrapped Micah from the stroller and started kissing his chubby cheeks, making him giggle. Propping Micah on her hip, she went around the counter, and they disappeared into the kitchen, leaving Rex standing there alone holding his blanket, hand on the handle of the stroller.

Rex let out a laugh and shrugged, turning towards the tables, all but one table occupied. There at the table were Harlow and Tyson. Harlow's blue eyes twinkled at the sight of him as he strolled over and nodded to an open chair across from where they sat, asking permission to join their duo.

"Go ahead." She replied.

Rex parked the stroller to the side, pulled out the diaper bag and settled in the seat next to him, he let out a long exhale. Meeting Harlow's amused expression, he turned his gaze to Tyson, who had according to the cupcake wrapper, cake crumbs and chocolate icing rimming his mouth, had obviously enjoyed a chocolate cupcake. "Hey there, Ty," he said, putting his fist out to bump. Tyson immediately bumped it and said, "T-Rex."

"That's right!" he exclaimed as his eyes drifted back to Harlow. "What brings you to Primrose?"

"Picking up treats for the coffee shop." She replied, picking up a glass of ice water on the table and taking a sip, then setting it down, tracing patterns in the condensation on the glass. "Cute baby," she commented, glancing towards the kitchen door. "I assume he's not yours."

"Rami's actually." He replied. "He and his wife Savanah needed a night out, so I offered to babysit. I am on Uncle Rex duty tonight."

Harlow was about to speak when the kitchen door swung open, Marnie carrying a cooler bag full of bakery boxes and striding over to Harlow, a happy Micah on her hip, gnawing happily on his fist. She set down the cooler bag next to Harlow and gave Micah one last kiss on the cheek before she handed him to Rex and returned to the counter to help some new customers that had just entered the bakery.

* * *

HARLOW WATCHED as Rex settled the adorable baby boy in his lap and reached over to the diaper bag, pulled out a snack cup with rice puffs and handed it to the infant. The sweet little boy with big brown eyes stuffed his already wet hand into the cup, taking out a handful and stuffing them into his mouth in a big drooly mess. Without missing a beat, Rex grabbed a spit up cloth off the handle of the stroller and wiped the drool off his dripping chin. He glanced up at her and let out a little chuckle as he said cheekily, "Micah is teething, so we have more drool than a St. Bernard at the moment."

Harlow let out a loud guffaw, louder than she intended as she took in the sight of her once bad ass boyfriend, so sweetly caring for the baby boy. Tyson climbed off his chair and rounded the table, standing next to Rex and reaching for the baby's hand, resulting in the baby boy giving him a gummy grin. They sat there for several minutes, no words said, as she watched her son play with the infant and she thought her heart might burst from the adorable sight. Her eyes met Rex's, and her heart skipped a beat as he flashed her a look that she was sure said, *this is what I want*. She shook her head nervously, picked up her ice water and took a long drink, needing to cool the longing she saw in his eyes. Rex's intense blue gaze was locked on her, which made her both anxious and intrigued, so she replied. "You're good with kids."

"I like them, and they seem to like me," he offered, running his hand over Micah's head with affection. "I hope to one day have some of my own."

Harlow could literally feel her ovaries perk up and body vibrate with his words, and she had to take a deep inhale to steady her nerves as she asked boldly, "Are you seeing anyone now?"

"No, I haven't dated since..." He didn't continue, but she read between the lines.

"Why?" she asked, honestly curious as she leaned forward and rested her elbows on the table.

He shifted in his seat, obviously taking his time to formulate his answer as he opened his mouth to speak. "I'm almost 31 years old and I'm an addict in recovery. It's not an easy thing to bring up in conversation, and with who I am, it's not something I can hide either. When I start dating again, I want to be in a place where I know I won't bring any chance of relapse into a relationship. My addiction will always be a part of my history, and I will always be ashamed of it, but I want to know it will not be a part of my future," he said, his gaze serious and intense. "The next woman I date is going to be the one. I want to get married, have a family and live a good life. I'm not going to date just to date. I'm going to date with the intention of it being forever."

Harlow's mouth was dry, not realizing she had been holding her breath as he poured his deepest intentions out to her. She swallowed hard, his words boring into her soul as she searched his eyes only to be met with honest sincerity. *Who is this man? Such a complete contrast from the man I knew and yet so much like Rex it both perplexes and interests me.* The realization that she wanted to see so much more of the first man to shatter her, confusing her heart.

CHAPTER 3

 alking into the Meeting Grounds, Rex spotted Jeremy immediately in the back and raised his hand in acknowledgment. His gaze drifted over to the coffee bar, and as he approached, Harlow's beautiful blonde hair came into view. She was crouched down, and he watched her fiddle with something under the sink as he waited patiently until she was done.

She popped up, turned around and gasped in surprise, clutching her chest, making him laugh. "How long were you there?" she asked, her face turning red as a smile curled her lips.

He looked at his watch and cocked an eyebrow at her. "Two minutes, give or take," he replied as his eyes drifted down to where she was fiddling. "Is there something wrong under the sink there?"

She let out a long sigh as she answered, "Yeah, I need to call a plumber, and I think he needs to replace a pipe under there. This is an old building, and it keeps leaking. I can't seem to stop it. It's just a small leak now, but small things get bigger, and I don't want to flood my coffee shop." She explained, exasperation in her tone.

Rex glanced down at the pail under the sink, used to catch the slow drops, and he met her gaze. "I have a meeting now, but I can fix it later tonight, if you want. It looks like a pretty basic fix, to be honest."

"Really?" she replied, reaching for a takeout cup and gesturing to it, asking if he wanted some coffee and acknowledging his nod. "I mean, I can't afford much these days, as I sunk everything into renovating this place, so I can't pay you."

"I would never ask you to," he replied, taking the cup from her hand, letting his fingers brush hers. A spark surged between them, and he looked up, meeting her beautiful blue eyes. "Isn't that what friends do? Help each other."

She pulled her hand away, and he could see from her expression she felt that bolt of electricity too. She grabbed a dishcloth and started wiping a small drip of coffee that had landed on the counter. Rex reached out and stopped her, causing her eyes to slowly raise to meet his.

"Seriously, I would be happy to help you, Harlow," he replied, brows drawn together and sincerity in his tone. "I hope we're friends, or did I assume wrong?"

She put her other hand on top of his and caressed it ever so slightly before her eyes met his. "Yes, Rex, we're friends, and thank you."

A grin tugging at his lips he put money down on the counter to pay for his coffee, as usual, far more than was necessary and flashed her his handsome smile, as he strode towards the back room, feeling her eyes on him as he went.

* * *

HARLOW WATCHED as Rex walked away, and she found herself taking in his appearance with admiration. He was slimmer and fitter than she remembered him, and his style had changed a lot. He was always dressed in this bad boy rocker edge, all leather, metal and rocker shirts. Now he was so much more understated, shirts more fitted to his trim frame and jeans hugging the asset she always had a fondness for, his tight butt.

She must have been staring at his retreating figure embarrassingly long, as she didn't hear Holly approach. Her eyes followed Harlow's, and she let out a little giggle. "He's definitely good looking." she said, making Harlow jump back and clutch her chest. *I have to stop being so jumpy.* She met Holly's gaze, her face blooming red from being caught ogling and Holly laughed as she added, "I mean in an older guy kind of way, of course. Do you two have a history together? I got that vibe last time he was here."

"We dated for like 3 years in high school." Harlow replied. "But back then he was an over-the-top rock star with a blue mohawk."

"Cool." Holly replied, nodding her head in approval. "Someone was in here the other day after he left and said he is a drummer in a famous rock band."

"Yeah, Prairie Sound. They hit it big, going viral, about six years ago, but I remember when they were just a bunch of guys playing covers in a garage." Harlow replied.

"Oh, I know those guys! They're pretty good!" Holly replied, giving her a nudge and walking past her to gather a few cups left on a table. "My mom loves them."

Thanks kid. As if I didn't feel old already.

* * *

THE NIGHT WAS warm and humid, with the promise of a thunderstorm in the air. Rex pulled up to the front of Meeting Grounds, parallel parking his Jeep and grabbing his toolbox from the passenger seat along with some replacement pipes he picked up at the hardware store. Walking to the door, the closed sign was up, and he glanced inside to see Harlow with a broom in hand close to the coffee bar. He knocked loudly, startling her, and waved at the door, holding up the toolbox for her to see. She flashed him a smile of recognition as she strode towards the door and flipped the lock to let him inside.

"I got everything I need here to fix that pipe," he said, meeting her gaze and holding up his toolbox and the various pipes in his hand. "Wasn't sure what I needed, so I brought everything."

She shook her head, but he could tell by the smile tugging at her lips that she liked the fact that he was taking this little job for her seriously. Leading him over to the coffee bar, he crouched down, inspecting the pipe and looked up at her with a grin. "As I suspected, this is an easy fix."

After asking her to shut the water off, he set to work,

removing the leaky pipe, and fitting a new one in its place. While he worked, she finished her end of day clean-up, yet he could sense her checking him out from time to time, or perhaps she was just checking his progress. He liked to think it was the first.

He reappeared from under the sink and found her watching him as she leaned over the counter on the other side on her tiptoes. Her eyes met his, their blue twinkling in the dim light of the closed coffee shop. "Are you done?" she asked curiously.

Rex nodded, hopping to his feet as he asked, "Can you turn on the water?" She disappeared, the sound of the pipes whining his indication that she had done as he asked. He inspected his work and smiled. "Perfect fix."

Standing up and brushing off his clothes, Harlow was already there by his side. Unexpectedly, she wrapped her arms around him in a hug and gave him a tight squeeze. He was so surprised he hesitated a moment and then reciprocated, wrapping his arms around her. She felt so good in his arms, the feeling of her body wrapped around his bringing on a wave of memories. She smelled like vanilla and a hint of coffee, and he found himself taking a deep indulgent inhale of her hair as its soft strands tickled his chin. Pulling away, she looked up at him, her hands still on his waist and his hands on her shoulders.

"Thank you." She said with so much gratitude in her eyes.

He smiled down at her, her blue eyes twinkling, and he couldn't help but think how easy it would be to lean down to kiss those pretty lips again. *No Rex.* His internal voice chided. *You aren't ready for that. You need more time.*

He stepped back, giving her a quick smile, and reached for his toolkit as he replied in a rather bad British accent, "My work, fair lady, is done."

Harlow threw her head back in laughter, her giggle sounding like music to his ears. He always loved her laugh; it was uninhibited and contagious. "Thank you, gallant knight." She replied, grabbing her purse from a shelf under the register and leading the way out from behind the coffee bar towards the door.

Rex followed, his eyes drifting over her back and down to the sway of her hips. Harlow was curvier now, and the hot-blooded man in him couldn't help but appreciate it. He swallowed hard as he asked, "So where is Ty tonight?"

"My parents took him over for a sleepover." She replied, offering him a sweet smile. "I get a rare night off from Mom duty."

He hesitated at the door, taking in her comment, and not wanting their time together to end this soon. "Have you eaten yet?" he asked. "I mean, have you had dinner?"

"No. I was going to have a sandwich or something when I got home," she replied.

"How does poutine at Sal's Fry Shack sound?" he asked, raising a curious brow at her. "I know it's still open for another hour."

Harlow rolled her eyes back, mouthing the word "yum." as she exclaimed. "I haven't had Sal's poutine in years!"

"Then let me treat you," he said. "You've been on your feet all day, and you deserve to relax and enjoy something indulgent."

She put her hand on her hip and cocked it to the side, the look of her so adorable he wanted nothing more than to pull her into him and kiss her breathless as she said, "Let me get this straight, you come here, fix my sink free of charge and now you want to buy me dinner?"

"Sounds about right," he replied with a chuckle. "Isn't that what friends do?"

She let out another giggle and chided, "Rex Johnson, I think we need to discuss the definition of friendship."

He cocked an eyebrow at her and smirked, "Harlow Ford, we can discuss whatever you want, but let's do it with a large order of dirty poutine from Sal's."

"Deal," she said, unlocking the door and gesturing for him to exit the coffee shop as she followed and locked the door behind her.

THE FRY SHACK was within walking distance, so Rex and Harlow strolled down the street side by side. St. Augustine was relatively quiet for a Friday night with only a few pedestrians taking in Main Street as the dark storm clouds loomed overhead. The humidity was thick, and Harlow could feel a sheen of sweat start to form on her skin as they crossed the street to be met by the sign of the famous seasonal hangout. Several groups of teens and twenty somethings were gathered by the picnic tables, and they looked up as they approached. Harlow could overhear one of the twenty-something girls, say excitedly to her friend next to her, "That's the drummer from Prairie Sound."

Rex must have heard her too and stopped at the table, putting out his hand to her. "Indeed, I am. Rex Johnson, and you are?"

The girl nearly choked on her words as she stuttered out her reply, "Katie."

"So nice to meet you, Katie," he replied, giving her a wink and reaching for her cell phone, which she had opened in front of her. He opened her camera app, leaned into her, and snapped a selfie. Handing her back her phone, the girl looked both shocked and about to blow a gasket. Then, in the coolest of ways, Rex flashed everyone at their table his sexy smile and strode back to Harlow, now waiting in line to place their orders.

"Well, if that wasn't a Rockstar move, I don't know what is," Harlow said, leaning into him and speaking out of the corner of his mouth. "Does that happen often?"

"All the time," he said with an amused smirk. "And now we can enjoy our dinner in peace."

Harlow looked up at him, thinking he was joking but was met by his intense gaze. His eyes told her he wanted all his attention to be on her tonight, and she couldn't help but feel her heart flip at the thought.

Takeout containers in hand, they spotted the only available picnic table at the end furthest away from the other patrons. Harlow slipped onto the bench, the heavenly smell of cheese curds, rich thick brown gravy, and deep-fried homemade french fries permeating the air around them. Eagerly she flipped open the container, closed her eyes and inhaled the delicious smell deeply. When she opened her eyes, Rex was watching her, his blue eyes dancing with delight.

"I forgot your ritual," he commented.

"My ritual? What ritual?" she asked, volleying back to him and knitting her brows together in question.

"Every time we had Sal's poutine, you would open the container, close your eyes and smell them before you would pick up your fork and start eating," he replied with a laugh. "I always thought it was the most adorable thing."

Harlow's cheeks bloomed red as she picked up her fork and loaded it up, making a show of shoving a big messy bite in her mouth, the gravy pooling in the corners of her lips.

Rex threw his head back and laughed. "You, Harlow, are the best."

"Shut up." She mumbled with her mouth full, her arms circling her takeout container protectively. "And let me enjoy my poutine."

Rex laughed again, the rich timbre of his voice making goosebumps form on her skin as he picked up his fork and dug in too.

* * *

HARLOW POPPED the last fry in her mouth, scraping the container clean, capturing the last of the gravy and cheese on her fork. "That was ah-mazing!" she exclaimed. "I didn't realize how hungry I was."

"You must work long hours," he observed, flipping his empty takeout container closed and meeting her gaze.

"Yeah, but I love it." She replied with a contented smile. "I mean, it's not like I'm not exhausted every day, but it was my vision and it's happening, so there are sacrifices."

"What was your vision exactly?" he asked, leaning in with curiosity.

She paused for a moment to formulate her answer as her gaze focused on Rex. "I wanted it to be a safe, friendly place, where people could come without judgement and I wanted it to be a meeting place, hence why I have the back of the coffee shop for that purpose."

"I love the idea and of course, I think it's amazing, but why just addictions meetings? I mean, Jeremy told me that the space in the back is reserved exclusively for SMART Recovery and any other meeting run by the Addictions Foundation here in St. Augustine."

Bringing her top lip between her teeth, she looked away, and he could see her head spinning with his question as she swallowed down and turned back to him. She met his eyes, searching his gaze as if trying to determine if she could be honest with him, then let out a big sigh, a confession tumbling out that he wasn't expecting. "My late husband was an addict."

His stomach fell and his heart squeezed painfully as he sat up straighter, his expression turning serious, and he leaned in, lowering his voice. "I assumed he was your ex-husband. I'm so sorry for your loss." Knowing these words were not sufficient to describe how he felt about this information, he met her gaze, more questions rapidly populating in his head.

"We were separated; he had been served with divorce papers, but never had a chance to finalize our divorce. He overdosed before that could happen." She added, looking solemn and resolute.

Rex shook his head, obviously taking in what she had just shared. "Fuck, Harlow, I'm so sorry you had to go through that. I mean, I don't know if I have words, Harlow, I..."

"You don't have to say anything. It happened, and it was awful, and even though we weren't together at the time, I did love him and wanted him to seek help." She replied. "Whether we were together or not, I wanted him to be sober and here for Tyson in the future, but that's not how it ended, and I have to live with that every day."

"You sound like you're assuming responsibility for what happened to him. You know the only one to blame is the addict, right? We always have a choice," he replied. "I mean, I had a choice. I didn't have to take drugs and drink myself into a stupor, but I did, so no one is to blame for my addiction but me."

She stared at him, his words hanging in the air between them, and she blinked rapidly, her eyelashes fluttering and revealing tears ready to fall. She turned her body away from him, bowed her head, her golden blonde hair veiling her face, and her shoulders started to shake.

Rising from the picnic table, he came around to her side, taking a seat next to her, and putting his arm around her protectively, pulling her to his side. "Don't cry, Harlow. I hate to see you cry."

He glanced up and noticed they had drawn the attention of several of the patrons waiting for food, whom he could tell recognized him. He didn't want Harlow to be fodder for gossip, so he leaned in and said, "Can I drive you home?"

She wiped her tears with her palm, noticing people looking their way, and stiffened. "Sorry I drew attention to us," she whispered, her voice cracking with emotion.

Waving it off, he rose from the bench as he put his hand out to her. "Let's walk it off, and I'll take you home."

She gave him a faint smile and took his offered hand, helping her up. They discarded their takeout containers and slowly strolled away from the fry shack.

"Sorry, I got a little emotional there." She said, looking up at him sheepishly. "I honestly don't know what came over me. I mean, Brendon passed almost four years ago, and I've had a lot of time to sort out my thoughts on the whole thing. I've done therapy, so it's not like I haven't aired all my feelings and thoughts out on this. It's just he was Ty's dad, you know?"

Rex nodded, imagining if he were in her shoes how it would feel to lose someone that important to his life like that. He almost did the same thing to his family and friends and knew what fear was when he looked in their eyes. But to know your child was without a father because of his poor decisions made his heart ache for her and for her son. They walked in quiet contemplation towards his vehicle, simply being comforted by each other's presence until she broke the silence.

"You know, Rex, you've changed so much, it's like you're the same guy, but not." she said with a smile tugging on her lips.

"You mean I fucking grew up." he replied with a little chuckle.

"Ah, there's the guy I know!" she exclaimed, nudging his shoulder playfully.

They both laughed as they got to his Jeep in front of her coffee shop. He clicked the button unlocking it and opened her door for her. She gave him a grateful smile as she hopped in, and he rounded the Jeep, climbing into the driver's side. He watched as Harlow admired the slick interior and smoothed her hands down the leather seat. "Pretty slick wheels here, Rockstar."

He leaned back, turning his head towards her, his eyes serious as he took in her comment and replied, "You know it's all just hype, right? I mean, it's awesome, but it could all be gone tomorrow."

"Do you really think that?" she asked, mirroring him by leaning her head back on the headrest and turning to face him.

"I do, I mean I can't take anything for granted anymore," he replied. "I very nearly lost it all, and I can't dangle on the edge of that cliff anymore."

She squinted her eyes at him and let out a long exhale, offering him a playful grin. "Who are you and what have you done with Rex Johnson?"

He shook his head, laughed, and started the Jeep, pulling out onto the street as she directed him to her apartment, grateful to have her back in his life. Even if just as a friend.

CHAPTER 4

Harlow woke with a start, hearing her phone buzz on her nightstand. She had been in such a deep sleep; it took her a moment to orient herself. Sitting up in bed, she reached for her cell phone and slid it open, clicking on a text from her mom, saying Ty slept well and was having breakfast and that she would drop him off later that afternoon. Harlow had taken a rare day off, Holly taking over the shift today along with a new part-time hire. There were no meetings scheduled, so they could close the back room and concentrate on the front of the shop. Harlow's phone dinged in her hand, and she glanced at the screen. A Facebook notification from The Real Rex Johnson. She smiled, swiping it and noticing a message request. Clicking on it, it said:

The Real Rex Johnson: *Do you want to be my friend?*

She let out a little giggle, feeling a little school girlish with her response rather than a 30-year-old single mom. With a cheeky grin, she responded:

Harlow Ford: *It depends. How do I know this is the "real" Rex Johnson?"*

The Real Rex Johnson: *Wouldn't you like to know?*

Three dots flashed at the bottom of their conversation and suddenly a picture of Rex appeared, leaning against what looked to be his kitchen counter, holding up a glass of orange juice without a shirt on. The angle of the picture gave Harlow the best view of his upper body and a tease of some washboard abs, and instantly her mouth went dry. *Well, good morning to me.*

A message popped up right after.

The Real Rex Johnson: *Proof enough?*

Harlow wasn't sure how to respond. Was he being playful as a friend or playful as someone trying to pique her sexual curiosity? Honestly, she wasn't sure. From what she knew of Rex before, she would have certainly thought the latter, but now the new Rex didn't push the boundaries and seemed genuine in his request for a friendship. Harlow decided to test the waters a bit.

Harlow Ford: *You look a little too buff for the Rex I remember, but it is possible you are him; I may need to look closer.*

The Real Rex Johnson: *LOL, sorry I just woke up. Seriously though, I had a good time with you last night and realized how much I missed having you in my life. I don't know about you, but our past relationship wasn't all about the crazy shit we did. I felt like you were my friend first and foremost, and I realized last night that I missed that.*

Harlow clutched her hand to heart, feeling the flutter she used to get around him, and responded:

Harlow Ford: *Yes, Rex, I would love to be your friend. I've missed our friendship too.*

* * *

REX WALKED into his gym just around the corner from his condo. He had started going there about a year ago and was finding the workout cathartic. Immediately he spotted Jeremy, who was standing in the front entrance, his phone in his hand.

"Hey man." Rex said as he approached.

Jeremy looked up, stuffing his phone into the pocket of his track pants. "Rex, are you ready to have your ass handed to you by this old man?" he asked, flexing his bicep and gritting his teeth at him.

Rex shook his head and laughed, knowing full well that Jeremy could kick his butt any day of the week. Truth was, Rex appreciated the friendship he had forged with Jeremy. He had become like an older brother to him and was so much more than just his sponsor. Jeremy had come with him on tour. He had been there through every craving to fall off the wagon and had become his biggest confidant. He was the only one in Rex's life who truly, honestly understood him and what he had been through, and he was beyond grateful to have him in his corner.

Striding towards his locker, he unloaded his wallet and keys and retrieved his boxing gloves, locking it behind him. Seeing Jeremy by the punching bag, he made his way over.

"I'll spot you first." Rex said, setting his gloves down as Jeremy pounded the bag, and Rex barely held on. "Got some frustration to get out there?" Rex asked with a laugh as Jeremy removed his gloves and reached for a towel to wipe his brow.

"Yeah," he replied, with exasperation in his tone. "Just the usual stuff, ex-wife trouble, bad-mouthing me to my kids. I mean, they're old enough to know who I am, and I don't hide my life struggles, but she always tries. It just makes me appreciate Carrie more, though. She accepts me, flaws and all." He said with a smile.

Rex mirrored him, thinking about the time he had spent with Jeremy and his longtime girlfriend, Carrie. They had been together for nearly a decade, and she was always his biggest support and champion. Carrie worked at the Addictions Foundation as a social worker, which was where they met, so she understood what he went through and loved him just as he was.

"You're lucky to have Carrie." Rex commented.

"I thank God, every day for her." Jeremy mused with a smile tugging at his lips. "Best thing that ever happened to me."

Rex reached for his boxing gloves and slipped them on, punching his hands together as he positioned himself on the other side of the bag and Jeremy held it. He threw a series of punches, his head reeling with questions.

"You seem distracted." Jeremy observed, furrowing his brows and meeting his eyes. "Anything you need to talk about?"

Jeremy's intuition astounded him. "Sorry, I am, I guess."

"What's bothering you?" he asked, gesturing for him to take a seat on a nearby bench.

Rex followed him and took a seat as he removed his gloves, setting them down beside him and running his hand over his head.

Jeremy gave him a look, a mix of curiosity and concern, as he placed a reassuring hand on his shoulder, letting him know that he was listening.

"I was wondering when you knew you were ready to date again?" Rex asked, glancing up at his friend. "I mean, I've always treated women as objects. Like they were to be discarded. I was always drunk or high. I treated sex like it was the end-all and be-all. Like it was something I could take rather than appreciate, and I'm not proud of how I treated women," he went on. "I guess I'm wondering if or when I can trust myself not to treat a woman that way again. I mean, literally, the only girl I ever had real, honest feelings for was Harlow."

"Harlow, like the Harlow Ford from Meeting Grounds?" Jeremy asked in surprise. Rex nodded. "I thought I sensed something there," he added. "Did you two date?"

"Three years in high school." Rex answered.

"That's a long time." Jeremy replied, his brows drawing together in question. "What happened?"

"I got high and cheated on her at a party." Rex replied, looking shamefully down at his hands.

Jeremy's back straightened, and he winced. "I bet you got caught too, right?"

"I did." Rex replied, cupping his head with his hands. "To this day, she is the best thing that ever happened to me.

"Wow!" Jeremy exclaimed, seemingly taken aback by

Rex's confession. "Okay, well, first, you're assuming responsibility for the breakup, which is good, as placing blame is counterproductive. You had a choice, and you made a poor one. Does she still have animosity towards you?"

"I don't think so, but I want to apologize, and tell her how sorry I am. If I'm being honest with myself, seeing her again has stirred up all the same feelings I had before," he continued, pouring out his thoughts. "I'm just so scared I'm going to hurt her again and that she deserves so much better than me."

"Did you love her back then?" Jeremy asked pointedly.

"I don't think I loved anything but my drum set back then. I did care for her deeply, like I would have done anything for her. But honestly, I think I was too self-absorbed and immature to truly be in love."

"Do you think she loved you?" he asked.

"No question." Rex answered quickly.

Jeremy squeezed his shoulder, and he turned his head to face him. "You'll know when the time's right for you. Harlow is a special person. If you knew her story, you would know you need to proceed with caution. She has lost a lot and has her son to think of."

"I know it's stupid to think that she would give me another chance, isn't it? She told me about her husband and about losing him to an overdose. The thought of bringing her back into that world again scares the shit out of me, and I couldn't do that to her and Ty." he replied, feeling emotion rise in his chest. "I just don't want to fuck it up with her again if I'm given a second chance."

"The fact that you're thinking like this is already

showing me that you are getting there, Rex. When do you feel you will be ready for a serious relationship again?" he asked.

"When I'm done with SMART Recovery." Rex replied, looking down at his hands. "I want my addiction to be part of my past before I pursue her."

"That's a smart and logical decision." Jeremy replied, rising from the bench. "Honestly, there is no handbook for all this, Rex. But you needed to stop doubting yourself. I've never worked with anyone more committed to recovery than you, and truthfully, you're on your way to a life free of your addiction."

Rex looked up at him, his words sinking in. "Do you really think so?"

"I know so, man," he said, meeting his eyes. "When you finally decide to date, whether it be Harlow or anyone else, I know you're going to treat them right. Do you want to know why?" Rex nodded as Jeremy tapped his chest. "Because you have a big heart."

Rex felt his words deeply as he cleared his throat, tamping down the rising emotion, he reached for his boxing gloves and rose from the bench. "Spot me again?"

Jeremy gave him a knowing nod and clapped him on the back, his advice a bandage on the wound of Rex's regretful heart.

* * *

RUSHING BETWEEN THE TABLES, Harlow smiled at some patrons as they dropped their empty cups off at the coffee bar and headed towards the door. Grabbing a cloth, she rounded the counter and wiped down tables as she heard the door chime and in walked Rex Johnson. He had a gym bag slung over his shoulder and was wearing basketball shorts and an athletic t-shirt that clung to his toned physique. *Wow.*

His eyes scanned the space, and as they settled on her, his lips curved into a smile. *Seriously, that smile.* She swallowed nervously, very aware of how his simple presence did crazy things to her mind and body. Approaching him, he cocked an eyebrow at her as he said, "Hello friend."

"Why hello there," she replied, feeling flirty for the first time in years as she brazenly trailed her gaze over his body. "Where were you coming from?"

He held up his bag as if she hadn't seen it. "The gym. Jeremy and I work out a few days a week."

She nodded suddenly feeling self-conscious thinking about the loose post pregnancy belly that she hated and how her only workout was chasing after Ty at the playground. She smoothed down her apron and gave him a quick smile as she rounded the counter to face him. "Can I get you your usual?"

"Do I have a usual already?" he asked playfully.

She rolled her eyes as she grabbed a takeout cup, filling it with coffee and popping on a lid. "You, my friend, have the easiest order ever to remember."

He laughed deeply, the rich tone of his voice making her vibrate deep down to her core. "Touche," he replied with a sexy wink as he strode over to the green couch and took a seat in the same place he'd sat the day they first saw each other. He reached into his gym bag, pulling out a book. Shaking her head, she laughed internally as the Rex she knew barely opened a textbook in high school. Honestly, now that she thought of it, she wasn't sure how he had managed to graduate from high school. The sight of him sitting in her humble coffee shop, reading a book, was completely out of character for the boy she once knew.

Trying to ignore his presence and failing miserably, she bustled around cleaning tables and helping patrons, and as the rush died down, her curiosity got the better of her and she rounded the coffee bar approaching him. Leaning over the couch, she watched him a moment and Rex looked up from his book, a smile tugging at his lips.

"Are you going to watch me read?" he asked, setting the book down on his lap.

"I might." She replied with a giggle. "I don't think I've ever seen you with a book. What are you reading there?"

He held up the book titled "Get Out of Your Own Way: Overcoming Self-Defeating Behavior".

Her brows furrowed as she commented, "That's some deep reading for a weekday afternoon. Is this a pleasure read, or a read for purpose?"

"Purpose," he replied, smoothing his hand over the cover. "Something I need to work on."

Harlow felt unexpected emotion rise in her chest as she rounded the couch and took a seat at the other end, her eyes on him as he continued, "I want to be a better person and forgive myself for all the fucked-up things I've done. That's been one of the hardest things for me. Not sure I can forgive myself yet..." he started, glancing down at the front of the book again, then he raised his beautiful blue eyes slowly to meet hers, sadness in their depths.

"...for all the people I hurt." Harlow searched his gaze, his comment a broad one, but seeming to speak directly to her. "I have a world of regret I need to reconcile, and honestly, some days it's all just too overwhelming to think about all the people that were scarred by my poor choices."

Harlow moved closer to him, drawn to him like a magnet, wanting, no, needing to be next to him as her throat tightened painfully. Seeing him like this, alive and vibrant but so broken inside, was almost too much to bear. She put her hand on his, and his eyes rose to meet hers as she asked, "You know I don't hate you, right?" His eyes brimmed with unshed tears, and she could see them glisten as she continued. "I'm not going to lie to you and tell you that I didn't," she added. "After I caught you with Tess, I both hated you and loved you all in one breath. It really confused my heart and, yes, it messed me up for a while. But Rex, you need to know I don't feel that way now. You're a good man; I can see that, and I have no regrets about the years we spent together. Looking back, the good memories far outweighed the bad ones for me."

"We had some really great times together." He replied with a smile tugging at his lips.

"We did," she mused. Do you remember all those drives we used to take, blasting Skid Row, "I'll Remember You" and singing at the top of our lungs?"

"That was a badass song," he replied, the fond memory washing over him.

"It's still my favorite." They both said in unison, making them laugh nostalgically as they settled in next to each other on the couch. They grew quiet, both with big smiles on their faces as a rush of memories surfaced.

Harlow let out a whistle as she added, "Those were some wild, hormone-induced times too, I tell you." She replied, pulling her hand away and instantly feeling her body warm at the memory of their combustible physical chemistry.

His brows furrowed with her words, and he leaned into her, a question on his lips. "I never hurt you back then, did I? I mean, we were a little out of control."

Waving off his question, she rose from the couch as several patrons entered the shop. Looking down at him and meeting his gaze, she answered his question. "Rex, I was always a willing participant."

He nodded, the apprehension in his eyes fading and he smiled as she walked away.

CHAPTER 5

*P*ulling into Rami's driveway, Rex parked, grabbed his extra pair of drumsticks off the passenger seat and made his way into the studio. As he entered, he was met by Rami, Layne and Juli along with 18-month-old Sebastien and soon to be 6-year-old Tabitha.

"Uncle Rex!" Tabitha squealed, running towards him, and nearly knocking him down.

"Hey there, princess!" he exclaimed, crouching down, and wrapping her in a big hug. Sebastien, with his shock of blonde hair, appearing behind her, shyly peering at Rex. "Seb, my man," he said, putting his fist out for a bump. Sebastien smiled and instead of bumping his fist joined his sister in tackling Rex to the ground as he tickled them both, their giggles echoing through the studio.

"Tabs and Seb!" Layne scolded with a laugh. "Let Uncle Rex get up."

The kids both climbed off him, letting him sit up and meet their gaze as he said in a low, ominous voice. "Papa has spoken."

They both ran off towards the couch in the corner and started jumping on it like it was a bouncy house.

"I better get these two crazies home before they tear this place apart." Juli said, rounding Tabitha and Sebastien up and looking towards Rex. "Are you coming to the BBQ tomorrow afternoon?"

"Yes, are you coming to my birthday party, Uncle Rex!" Tabitha asked, jumping up and down, her little brother following suit.

"I wouldn't miss it," he replied, gripping her head in his hands, and leaning down to kiss her on the forehead. "What do you want this year? Perhaps a gigantic teddy bear or hmmm... maybe a pony?"

"Don't you dare, Rex Johnson!" Juli replied, giving him a chiding look, and Tabitha put her lip out in a pout.

"Sorry, kiddo." He shrugged with a laugh. "Our plan has been foiled."

Everyone laughed as Juli exited the studio, the kids in tow. Suddenly, a thought dawned on him, and he turned to Layne. "Do you mind if I invite someone to the party?"

"Like a date?" he asked, folding his arms over his chest.

"No, like a friend and her son," he replied. "He's a bit younger than Tabitha, actually."

"Yeah, sure." Layne answered. "The more the merrier. But who is this friend of yours?"

"Harlow Ford."

Layne's eyes widened, and he leaned in, asking, "Harlow Ford?"

Rex nodded.

"So, you two are friends now?" Rami asked with a huge grin.

"We are, and I think it would be a nice surprise for Juli and Harlow to be reunited." Rex answered.

Layne's lips turned up in a nostalgic smile, remembering how close the two girls had become back in high school, and exclaimed, "I think that would be amazing!"

"Let me send her a message then." Rex said as he pulled out his phone and swiped it open. He could feel their eyes on him as he sent her a quick message asking her what she was doing tomorrow afternoon. Rex looked up from his phone and was met with their big goofy grins just as Steve walked in looking speculatively between them all.

"What's going on?" he asked curiously, his eyes sparkling with amusement at the scene.

"Harlow Ford." Layne answered.

Steve's eyes darted over to Rex as he exclaimed, "No fucking way!"

* * *

IT HAD BEEN AN EXHAUSTING DAY, and it was only 1 p.m. Harlow's feet hurt and her back hurt, and she was seriously starting to wonder if this whole owning her own business was a smart decision. Meeting Grounds had become a hot spot in town, and although she was excited about the loyal business coming through the doors daily, she knew she couldn't keep up with the hours she was currently keeping. It had become apparent that she needed to add more staff or at the very least one more fulltime employee, so her profit margins didn't decrease too much. Truth was that she was barely getting by despite the constant influx of business, and she wasn't sure how much longer she could keep Meeting Grounds afloat.

Setting some mugs into the sink, she felt her phone vibrate in her apron and pulled it out, swiping open the notification.

The Real Rex Johnson: *What are you doing tomorrow afternoon?*

Harlow Ford: *I don't know, working probably.*

The Real Rex Johnson: *Do you think Holly could cover for you?*

Harlow Ford: *Why?*

The Real Rex Johnson: *I want to take you and Ty somewhere.*

Harlow Ford: *Where?*

The Real Rex Johnson: *You ask too many questions.*

Harlow Ford: *Is that a problem?*

The Real Rex Johnson: *No, but I think you'll like the surprise. Do you trust me?*

Harlow Ford: *I think the question here should be, can I trust you?*

The Real Rex Johnson: *You can trust me. I promise you're going to love this surprise.*

She bit her lip, a smile trying to escape as Holly entered the coffee shop, wrapping her apron around her waist and offering Harlow a knowing smile.

"Talking to Hottie McDrumsticks again?" she asked with a wink.

"Hottie McDrumsticks?" Harlow echoed with a giggle.

"Yeah!" she exclaimed with a cheeky grin. "He's hot, and he's a drummer in a band, hence Hottie McDrumsticks."

Harlow giggled again and shook her head, then asked, "Do you want to pick up an extra shift tomorrow?"

"Yeah, sure!" she replied happily as she grabbed a cloth and rounded the counter.

Harlow wasn't sure what she would do without Holly. She looked down at her phone, another message from Rex:

The Real Rex Johnson: *What do you say? Shall I pick you and Ty up at 2 p.m.?*

Harlow Ford: *Looking forward to it.*

REX TURNED onto Harlow's Street, the mid-century houses and large oak trees shadowing his path. This was a pretty part of old St. Augustine, and he always liked how the yards were blanketed by leaves in the fall. Her apartment building coming into view, he saw her and Ty sitting on the front steps waiting for him. He pulled up and got out, rounding the front of his Jeep as they made their way down the front walkway towards him.

He crouched down immediately and put his fist out to Ty, who gave him a shy smile and bumped it. "How are you doing, little man? Are you ready for a fun afternoon?"

Ty smiled as he reached for Harlow. Harlow was holding a booster seat for the car and had what appeared to be a large backpack slung over one shoulder. Upon noticing she was loaded down, Rex sprung up and reached for the car seat. "Let me help you with that."

She gave him a grateful look as she took Ty's hand and watched with interest as Rex made short work of installing the car seat and put his arms out for Ty. "Your seat is ready. Can I buckle you in?"

Ty let go of Harlow's hand, and she watched as her son ran into Rex's arms. He picked him up, making a whirring sound of a plane, eliciting a giggle from Ty before setting him in the car seat and buckling him in. He closed the door and turned, Harlow still watching him.

"How did you know how to install his car seat?" she asked, with a mix of curiosity and mirth in her inquiring eyes.

Rex smiled and held his arms out wide. "You are looking at the one and only Uncle Rex here."

Harlow shook her head and let out a little giggle as he opened her door and held it as she got inside. Slipping into the driver's seat, he met her still curious gaze and looked behind him at Ty sitting happily in his car seat. His eyes drifted back to her as he took in how impossibly pretty she looked today. Her gorgeous golden hair cascaded just past her bare shoulders, which were freckled by the sun and shown off by the spaghetti-strap breezy sundress she wore the same color as her stunning blue eyes.

"You look beautiful today." He said simply as he saw the flash in her eyes and a blush of pink creep into her cheeks.

"Is it too much?" She asked, smoothing down the front of the dress.

"It's perfect," he replied, glancing back at Ty dressed in a blue t-shirt and navy cargo shorts, their outfits complementing each other. He couldn't help the wide grin taking over his face. Having them here in his vehicle, it felt like a family going on an outing or perhaps a day trip, and the thought of that made his heart swell with an unexpected happiness. Harlow's eyes met his, twinkling with amusement as she said, "I have so many questions."

A deep laugh rumbled from his chest as he replied, "I wouldn't expect anything less."

THEY PULLED off the main road that led to Primrose, kicking up gravel and dust as they went. "We're not going to Primrose?" she asked, taking in wheat fields and the large sign for Prairie Sky Acres. "Wait," she said, looking behind them as they turned at the intersection of the farm heading again to Primrose. "This is the way to Layne's parents' place."

"Ding ding ding ding!" he replied with a laugh. "Although it's Layne's place now."

"Really?" she asked as they got to another intersection, passing Hayden Hastings' large gorgeously renovated house. "Are we meeting the guys?"

"Yes." he replied, quickly glancing her way. "Them and their families. We have a celebration today."

She sat up taller in her seat and smiled excitedly as

they approached Layne's property and slowed down. Harlow took in the driveway full of cars as her eyes darted to the garage, which was once Prairie Sound's practice space. "The garage!" she exclaimed as he found a parking spot. "You guys don't still play there, do you?"

"No, Rami has this amazing state-of-the-art studio off his house in Primrose," he replied as he put his Jeep into park. She nodded, releasing her seat belt as she waited for him to get out and she followed. He immediately opened the back door and started unbuckling Ty and Harlow felt her heart skip a beat as she watched her son willingly go into Rex's arms. Her son was always a bit apprehensive around strangers, and for that she was thankful, but for some reason, from the first time he met Rex, his infatuation began. It was T-Rex this and T-Rex that. Rex had a way with people and always had. Even as a foul-mouthed, cocky teenager, one still couldn't help but like him. Yet now with his rough edges filed down to smooth corners, she couldn't believe how awesome he was with her son.

Rex set Ty down and Harlow took Ty's hand reaching for the backpack, but before she could grab it, Rex had it slung over his shoulder and was going to the hatch of his Jeep to retrieve probably the largest pink floral gift bag she had ever seen, stuffed full of pink, purple and blue tissue paper, dappled with glitter.

Harlow laughed as he grabbed the enormous bag and clicked a button to close the hatch. "What kind of celebration is this?"

"It's a celebration for a beautiful princess!" he announced, and Ty's eyes widened as he looked up at Harlow with excitement. "Let's go meet her."

They walked towards the house, and he led them around the side, the sound of music, giggles of children and laughter echoing across the yard. Rounding the side of the house, a gigantic bouncy house appeared in the backyard, and the smell of hotdogs and hamburgers wafted from the grill. She immediately recognized Layne. He was a little older and more filled out, but honestly looked exactly the same as he did at 17.

Everyone turned to them, and she looked around the crowd gathered on the deck until her eyes met the familiar big, beautiful brown eyes of someone she hadn't seen in 14 years. There on the back deck of Layne Stark's house was her high school friend, Juli Roth. Juli slowly made her way down the steps, passing Layne at the grill, her eyes wide and glistening with tears of recognition. "Harlow?" She asked, her accent thick and so familiar it made tears well up in Harlow's eyes. She glanced at Rex; his smile was wide as he gestured towards Juli. "Surprise," he said as he set the gift bag down and reached for Ty's hand. "Go ahead. I got Ty."

She turned to Juli, a few metres away from her, and ran towards her long-lost friend, crashing into her open arms. With tears streaming down their faces, they laughed through their joyful sobs as they held tight to each other. Juli pulled away, both women gazing fondly at each other at arm's length.

"I can't believe you're here, Juli. Are you visiting? I mean, how are you here?" Harlow asked, so many questions rushing through her head.

"I moved here 6 years ago. It's Juli Stark now. Layne and I are married." She replied with a shrug.

Harlow glanced around Juli, her eyes meeting Layne's as he approached them, and she glanced towards the deck to see Rami and Steve, both holding babies and coming down the steps with two beautiful women at their sides. Harlow glanced around as they neared her, taking in each of them, and wiped at the wetness on her cheeks, a flood of memories coming back to her.

Rex joined them, Ty clutching his hand tightly. "Harlow, you know the guys, but you haven't met their wives." He gestured to probably the most beautiful woman she had ever seen with long pink hair pulled up into a high ponytail, her hand resting on a tiny swell of a baby belly. "This is Savanah, Rami's wife." Savanah gave her a wave, and Rami wrapped his arm around her, giving her a loving glance as he held onto the baby boy she met at the bakery.

Harlow leaned in and gently brushed his chubby cheek. "Hello again, Micah." The baby gave her a gummy smile.

"This is Steve's wife, Emersyn." Rex gestured to a stunning ebony woman, petite in stature, like herself, with magnetic midnight eyes, and the most enviable head of ringlet hair. Steve towered over her, and yet somehow, she sensed that what Emersyn lacked in size, she made up for in personality.

"Hi, Harlow," she replied, her voice smooth like butter as she put out her hand in greeting.

Harlow took it and glanced up at Steve holding a baby girl, no more than a few months old. "Is this your daughter?" she asked, looking between Emersyn and Steve.

Steve nodded proudly as he replied, "This is our Belle."

Harlow approached the baby, putting her hand out, and the little one grabbed her finger, gripping it firmly. "She's precious."

Harlow stepped back, taking everyone in and shaking her head in disbelief as she laughed with tears in her eyes and exclaimed. "You all grew up! This is so surreal."

Everyone mirrored her laughter and nodded their heads in agreement as their eyes drifting down to Ty holding Rex's hand. Harlow's eyes followed them, and she moved to her son's side, smoothed down Ty's blonde hair and said, "This is my son, Tyson."

Just then a little girl, the spitting image of Juli, ran up, her face red and sweaty, and hair staticky from the bouncy house. She was wearing a big poofy tutu and a princess crown and had one of her front teeth missing. "Uncle Rexth!" she exclaimed, taking in the huge gift bag and glancing at Ty clinging onto Harlow now.

"Did you lose your front tooth?" Rex asked with amusement. "I just saw you yesterday."

She put her hand on her hip and cocked it to the side in a super sassy fashion. "If I don't losth them, Uncle Rexth I can't get my big teeth." She said, her tongue darting through the gap as she talked.

Rex let out a laugh and crouched down. "I brought you a new friend to play with," he said. "This is Tyson, or you can call him Ty."

Tabitha boldly approached Tyson and reached for his hand. "Hi Ty! I'm Tabitha, or you can call me Tabths. Let's go bounce." She said, dragging him away from Rex and Harlow. Ty glanced briefly behind him but willingly followed with the hugest grin on his adorable face.

"She's a miniature Juli," Harlow declared with a giggle as she wrapped her arms around Juli's waist and hugged her again. "Okay, I need the scoop on how you and Layne finally got back together."

Juli laughed as she exclaimed, "Harlow, you have so much to catch up on!"

CHAPTER 6

$\mathcal{H}$arlow leaned on the deck railing watching as Rex, Steve, Layne and Rami kicked a soccer ball around the yard, a swarm of kids chasing after them. Ty's blonde hair bounced as he ran with them, lost in the mix and smiling from ear to ear. Seeing her son so happy made her heart swell with joy. He had a few friends, mostly kids from daycare, but with no cousins and Harlow having few friends of her own now, it wasn't lost on her how much Ty needed a day like this.

"Ty is so sweet." Juli said, wrapping her arm around Harlow. "Does he look more like you or his dad? I know when I look at him, I see you."

"Both, actually." She replied, a grin tugging at her lips as she remembered Brendon fondly. "Everyone always tells me he looks like me, but I see a lot of Brendon in him too."

"Is his dad part of his life?" Juli asked pointedly. Juli was never one to mince words, was always straightfor-ward, and that was something Harlow appreciated about her friend. If she wanted to know, she was always bold enough to ask.

Harlow turned to meet her gaze. "Ty's dad passed away 4 years ago."

Juli's brows knit together, sympathy in her big expressive brown eyes as she placed her hand on her chest. "I'm so sorry, Harlow."

Harlow waved off her apologies, letting her know she was okay discussing her late husband. "Brendon and I were married for two years and were separated when he passed."

"Still, that's a lot to go through." Juli added, giving her a squeeze. "Was it sudden?"

"You could say that," Harlow replied, always hating telling this part of her story. "Brendon died from a drug overdose."

Juli stood up straighter, her eyes locked on Harlow's as she said, "Oh my God."

It was the response she expected, and yet, hearing her own story again and telling one of her dearest friends from the past about how her life turned out, made a large, painful lump form in her throat. Swallowing hard, she glanced out to see Ty tackle Rex to the ground as he held him up in the air, his giggle echoing across the expansive yard.

Juli's eyes followed her gaze as she leaned on the deck again and said, "Rex is good with him."

"Ty likes him." Harlow replied simply, watching Rex get to his feet and swing Ty around.

"Rex is going to be an amazing father someday." Juli added as they watched.

Harlow furrowed her brows, a question needing to be asked, but not knowing if she should go there. "Do you think Rex is ready for a relationship, a family or a commitment?"

"Personally, I think he is, but I still think he struggles to trust himself." Juli replied honestly.

Harlow turned to face her, more questions formulating in her head. "What do you mean by that?"

"I think he's afraid. I mean, he almost died; his life got so out of control." She shared. "Two years ago, at Tabitha's birthday party, we got the call that he was rushed to hospital, and from there we didn't see him for months."

"Where did he go?" Harlow asked curiously, gripping the sides of the railing.

"Rehab, right from the hospital. He was there for three months, and when he got out, he was like a shadow of himself." Juli said with a shake of her head. "He was thin and looked so incredibly tired, it was hard to believe it was the same man. The guilt and remorse for his past behavior ate at him. You could just see it. His spirit was completely broken."

"So, what got him to where he is today?" She asked, glancing over at him. "Why do you think he's ready?"

"Rex has done everything, and I mean everything, to prove to his family and to us that he has become a better man. He has done the 12-step program, which I know was excruciating for him. He has done therapy, both group and individual, and may still be doing that; I'm not sure. And now he's doing SMART Recovery, which I know he told Layne would help him transition to a normal life again and free him of his addiction. Not sure how that works, but from what I have read up on it, it sounds like this is the final step for him." She replied.

Harlow turned to watch Rex crouch down, wipe the dirt off Ty's face and give him a fist bump. "He's certainly not the guy I remembered, and yet, the old Rex is still there. Like a Rex whose edges have been smoothed down."

"That's a pretty great way to describe it, actually." Juli said with a laugh as they watched the four bandmates and brothers round up all the kids and make their way back to the deck.

Layne called out to Juli, "Is it cake time?"

Juli nodded and leaned into Harlow, speaking from the side of her mouth. "I refer to it as crash and burn time."

Harlow threw her head back with a laugh as she watched her friend disappear through the patio doors into the kitchen. She turned, Rex lifting Ty onto his shoulders as he strode over to her on the deck.

"Why hello there, pretty mama!" Rex said with a twinkle in his eye as Ty beamed from above him. With Ty on his shoulders, he was the perfect height to reach Harlow leaning on the deck. Rex leaned Ty into her so she could give him a quick peck on the lips.

"Are you having fun, Ty?" she asked, taking in his red sweaty face, sprinkled with dirt and a happy grin.

"Yes!" he exclaimed.

"Good, it's cake time."

"Ooo, cake time!" Rex said, licking his lips and giving her a wink as he lifted Ty from his shoulders and took his hand. "Come on, Ty! Let's see if we can get the biggest piece!"

With that she stood back, watching as Rex wiped down Ty's dirty cheeks and hands, as he held him while they all sang "Happy Birthday" so he could see Tabitha blow out the candles and how they shared the biggest slice of chocolate cake both smiling as they talked. All the while, Harlow watched with wonder as glimmers of hope settled in her heart.

* * *

THE DRIVE BACK TO ST. Augustine was a quiet one. Ty was passed out in his seat, his blonde head dropping to the side as he slept. Rex glanced over to Harlow, who was gazing out the passenger window, watching as the stars started to come out and speckle the sky.

"Did you like your surprise?" Rex asked, glancing over to her quickly, a huge smile covering his face.

"I did," she replied, shifting her body to face him. "I still can't believe Juli and Layne are married and have this beautiful family together."

"Sometimes first love is the one that sticks." Rex said, stealing a glance at her. "Sometimes it takes losing the best thing in your life to understand what you let go of."

The cab grew silent, but he could feel her eyes watching him as he drove closer to St. Augustine, and he could almost hear her brain working through his comment. But instead of asking him to clarify, which he thought she might do, she turned and continued to look out the window at the stars with a contented smile on her face.

Pulling up to the front of her apartment building, Rex parked and unbuckled his seat belt, turning to meet her eyes. "Can I help you get everything inside?"

She nodded, and he climbed out of the Jeep, rounding the vehicle and opening the passenger door. Harlow reached for the backpack, slipping it on and made quick work of unbuckling Ty, his body wrapping around her with a groggy groan, and his sleepy head resting on her shoulder.

"I'll get the car seat," he whispered as he reached into the vehicle and made short work of uninstalling the seat, carrying it and following Harlow to the front door of the building.

"Can you reach into the front pocket of the backpack and take out the keys?" she asked, her voice low. "The building key is the blue one."

He nodded and opened the door for them as he followed them inside and up the stairs to the second floor. She led him down the hall almost to the end and stopped at her apartment door. "The yellow one, please." She said with a whisper, and he did as she asked, opening her apartment door.

As they entered, he took in her space, the main living room and kitchen space open to each other. It was small, cozy, and tidy, his eye immediately going to an eclectic collage of colorful drawings and pictures on the wall hanging over a small plush sectional couch.

"Can you put the car seat in my room?" Harlow whispered. "It's the last one at the end of the hall."

He nodded, following her down the hall and watching her detour into the bathroom with Ty. Entering her bedroom; he flicked on the lights and took in the space. Her bedroom was small, almost entirely eaten up by a queen-size bed dressed in a simple floral bedspread. A bookshelf full of books stood in the corner, and on the opposite side was a closet that took up almost the entire wall. Noticing a free spot in the corner, he set down the car seat and glanced around her space. On the wall across from her bed were two pieces of wood with strings attached end to end in several rows and mini clothespins attached to photos. Surveying the display with interest, he smiled as he took in the candid photos of Ty. His bright grin and twinkly blue eyes, gracing every picture. Some of the pictures were of Harlow and Ty, their smiles so beautiful it made his heart flutter. Running his hand over his chin, he couldn't help but wonder what it would look like to have pictures of all three of them here on display.

Tonight, he got a taste of what being part of a family could look like. He and Ty had bonded, and glancing over at Harlow, he could tell she had noticed. Stealing glances throughout the day, he felt her eyes on him as he played and took care of Ty at the party and, honestly; he loved every minute of it. Walking towards the door, he glanced back one more time, a smile tugging at his lips as he flicked off the light. Striding down the hall, he stopped at the door he assumed was Ty's bedroom and slowly opened the door a crack to take a peek inside. Harlow had dressed Ty in pajamas, was tucking him into bed and handing him a stuffed T-Rex. Rex smiled at the thought of that and caught her gaze as she turned to head out of the room. She glanced back at Ty with the dinosaur under his arm, and a grin bloomed on her face. Turning to face Rex she whispered, "It's his favorite."

Rex nodded with a grin as she slipped out of Ty's room and closed his door softly. They stood so close he could feel the heat coming off her body and transferring to him. Harlow looked up, her cheeks taking on a rosy hue as she asked, "Do you want to hang out here a bit with me? Perhaps watch a movie?"

"Yeah, that sounds nice," he said with a smile as he followed her down the hall to the kitchen/living room. Rather than following Harlow into the kitchen, he detoured into the living room, taking in her display on the wall, the realization of what she had on the wall making him smile.

"Are these all, Ty's drawings?" he asked, taking in each colorful house, animal, dinosaur and person.

"They are," she said proudly, reaching into the cupboard and pulling out two glasses and a box of microwave popcorn.

He brought his hand to his chin and squinted, pretending he was some art aficionado scrutinizing the artwork on the wall of a gallery. "You know, I think you have the next Picasso here."

Harlow let out a little giggle and put a bag of popcorn into the microwave, then reached into the refrigerator, pulling out a 2-litre bottle of Coca-Cola and pouring them each a glass. "I mean, he is the most talented kid in the world after all." Poking fun at the words most parents utter at least once about their child.

Rex laughed and glanced back at the display. "You, Harlow, are a great mom."

Turning back to her, she stood holding two glasses of coke, her grateful eyes meeting his. "Most days, I feel like I'm barely holding it together, but honestly, I do my best." She replied, with a slight crack in her words.

Did I strike a sensitive topic, or had she been touched by the compliment? The truth was, he marveled at how she did it all. Single mom, running a thriving business and doing serious good for the community in the process. She was a wonder to him and deserved all the praise he could give her and more.

"I just call it like I see it," he added with a playful wink.

Harlow smiled and handed him a glass, setting hers down on the coffee table as she rushed back to the kitchen and retrieved the popcorn, dumping it into a plastic bowl and coming back to the couch. They both sat, the bowl between them as she reached for the remote. He watched as she scanned the movies and settled on a classic, *Mission Impossible,* that instantly brought back memories. As the movie started, he kept stealing glances at her, wondering if it induced memories for her as well. They were about a half hour into the movie, the popcorn bowl now empty and Harlow curled up on the opposite end with her feet on the couch, when she said, "Isn't this the movie we had on the first time we..." her voice trailed off as that endearing rosiness blossomed on her cheeks again.

"I was wondering how long it would take you to realize that," he said with a low chuckle as he cocked his eyebrow at her. "Was this part of your plan to seduce me?"

He was sure she would laugh, but instead she sat up

straighter and looked him straight in the eye, asking boldly, "What if it was?"

"I would say we just rekindled a friendship right now, and I don't think we should blur those lines yet," he replied honestly.

She nodded, looking back at the screen, Tom Cruise doing some insane stunt for the camera, and said with a reminiscent sigh, "That was a fun night though."

"It was," he agreed, the night they lost their virginities to each other on the ratty basement couch. "I was too much of a horny teenager to make it special for you though. Looking back, I wish I held that moment with more weight, you know?"

Harlow turned to meet his gaze, her eyes dancing as a grin curled her lips. "It was perfect just the way it was. Besides, I do believe I was the one who made the first move that night."

Rex sifted through his memory bank to that night, both on the couch, his arm around her, as she met his eyes and took his other hand, guiding it up her skirt. His eyes darted to her as he said, "You naughty minx."

Harlow let out a giggle and shrugged as she set the popcorn bowl on the coffee table and reached for a throw pillow. Settling on the chaise, she laid her head down. As they watched the movie, his eyes kept drifting over to her, her eyes half-mast, blinking slowly and deliberately, until they finally closed, and he could hear her breathing deepen. He watched her for a long time, sleeping so soundly, her golden hair resting perfectly on her bare shoulders. *She's so beautiful,* he thought, taking in her long dark lashes fluttering now and then and pink pouty lips settled into a perfect bow. *How could I have not appreciated her back then?* With the feeling of self-deprecating regret and guilt washing over him, he noticed her shiver, and goosebumps forming on her bare arms. He glanced around the room, noticing a warm throw blanket on the chair next to the couch. Getting up, he reached for it, opening it wide and laid it on top of her, covering her bare arms and legs. Her pretty lips parted ever so slightly, and an audible sigh escaped as she snuggled into the blanket. Staring down at the angel he had discarded so easily 12 years ago, he leaned down and kissed her head, the softness of her hair feeling like silk against his lips. Settling back down on the couch, he flipped off the movie and the lights as he settled onto the other side of the couch, crossed his arms over his chest and watched as the moonlight from the window cast shadows on the sleeping beauty across from him. As he let his eyes drift closed, dreams of Harlow and Ty, all of them together, danced through his consciousness as a promise of what could be possible.

CHAPTER 7

Rex's eyes slowly cracked open, the light from the window cascading into the living room. His peripheral vision caught movement on the other side of the couch and immediately met Ty's curious blue gaze.

"Hey there, Ty. Good morning," he said, sitting up and feeling the ache in his muscles from falling asleep in an awkward position on their couch.

"Good morning." Ty said softly, holding out his stuffed T-rex to him and making him growl.

Rex let out a laugh and reached over, tickling the little boy and making him giggle. Glancing around, Rex asked, "Where's your mom?"

"In the shower," he said softly. Ty was so soft-spoken; it was part of what made him adorably sweet. Rex listened for a moment, hearing the spray of the water and the whine of the pipes. He nodded and smiled at Ty as he asked, "Can you get me some cereal?"

"Sure," Rex replied, rising to his feet and feeling way

older than his 30 years as he stiffly walked to the kitchen and Ty hopped onto a stool across from the peninsula. "Let's see what you've got here?"

"Above the fridge." Ty said quietly.

Rex nodded, opened the cupboard above the fridge to find three boxes of cereal and instantly grabbed the Fruit Loops, holding them up for Ty. "How did you know Froot Loops are my favorite?"

Ty giggled and replied, "They are my favorite too."

Rex gave him a grin as he searched the cupboards finding the bowls and pulling out two, he found the drawer with the spoons and poured them each a big bowl of Froot Loops, topping them with milk from the fridge, then handing Ty a spoon. "Now before we eat our cereal, we need to clink our spoons together to warn the cereal that we are coming for them."

Ty threw his head back in a big giggle, the sound so sweet to Rex's ears. "Is it because we are cereal monsters?"

"No. But we are cereal dinosaurs! I am T-Rex, and you are a Ty-rannosaurus." he said with a wink.

"That's the same dinosaur." He replied with a laugh. "You are funny, T-Rex."

Rex laughed too as they clinked spoons and scooped up the biggest spoonful that they could manage as they messily ate that first bite.

* * *

WRAPPED IN A TOWEL, Harlow stood just out of sight, peeking around the hallway, watching as Ty and Rex ate their bowls of cereal together. As they talked and laughed, she marveled at how their connection seemed so natural, and it made her smile. Rex was so cute and playful with Ty, and as she watched them, she couldn't help but think of Juli's words yesterday. *Rex is going to be an amazing father someday.* The thought of this being a normal day in their lives, Rex doting on Ty like he was his son, filled her with an overwhelming warmth and deep sense of yearning. She wanted this for Ty, for him to have a father figure in his life. *Perhaps they were friends now, but maybe in the future? Rex said yesterday that he didn't think they should blur the lines.* Despite his words, she could feel those familiar feelings and emotions resurface when she was with him and seeing him here, so amazing with her son; her heart couldn't help but feel hopeful for their future.

* * *

"WHAT DID YOU DO THIS WEEKEND?" Holly asked as she dried coffee mugs and put them back on the shelves.

"Rex took Ty and I to a birthday party for one of his bandmates' daughters." Harlow replied, feeling light and breezy this morning. "His bandmate and one of my best friends from high school that I hadn't seen in 14 years got married, and he surprised me by reuniting us. It was the sweetest thing."

"That sounds so sweet." Holly said, clutching her chest. "He's really getting under your skin, isn't he?"

A smile tugged at Harlow's lips, and she looked away. The truth was that Rex wasn't just getting under her skin. He was occupying her mind during the day and starring in her dreams at night. And his great way with Ty was beginning to make her fall for him.

Harlow glanced at the clock on the wall, noticing it was fast approaching time for the SMART Recovery meeting, which meant that Rex would be arriving any time. Just thinking about seeing him again made her heart race, and she could feel her breath labour. He was having a serious effect on her physically, and she needed to get herself under control. Just as she steadied herself, Rex walked in, looking impossibly hot, and her pulse spiked. *Why does he always have to look so good? Damn you, traitorous body.*

* * *

SAUNTERING over to the coffee bar, Rex met Harlow's gaze as a smile rose on his lips. "Hello there, friend," he said playfully as he gave her a wink. He could see her cheeks pinked with his words and the need to touch them and feel the heat there made his fingers tingle. His ability to so easily make her blush quickly becoming one of his favorite things.

"Hey!" she replied with a sweet smile as she grabbed a takeout cup, poured coffee into it and handed it to him.

He reached for it, his hand covering hers and lingering as their eyes met. The usual sizzle passed between them, and he could see in her eyes she felt it too. She cleared her throat nervously, slipped her hand away and grabbed a dishcloth as she rounded the coffee bar.

"Busy day today?" he asked, his brows furrowed as he tried to analyze her reaction to him.

"So busy," she replied. "I really need to bring on more staff, but the cost, honestly I'm not sure how to do it all."

Rex took in her words, now voicing what he suspected. She was treading water and barely keeping afloat. What she had created here was something special, her vision clear, but it was far too much for one person. She needed help, and he knew he could give it to her. You didn't grow up the son of a successful business owner and not pick up a few things, and if there was anyone he wanted to help, it would be Harlow.

"I have a meeting right now, but I have a few ideas that may help you." Rex said with a smile as he put his arm around her shoulders and gave them a reassuring squeeze. "Let's talk after my meeting." Her eyes met his with curiosity, and he leaned in, whispering, "It's going to be okay." With those words, her shoulders eased, and he gave her a quick smile as he made his way to the back for his meeting.

* * *

THE SLIDING door of the back room opened, and people filed out, some looking weary-eyed and emotionally spent, others like a weight had been lifted from their shoulders. Harlow always liked to watch them, wondering what their story was and feeling good about what she was doing here at Meeting Grounds.

After Brendon's overdose, she moved back to St. Augustine to be closer to her parents and knew she needed help to sort through her feelings on everything. With the help of the Addictions Foundation and therapy, she was able to overcome so much of the guilt and hurt from loving someone with an addiction and knew first-hand the power of these meetings. Being able to give back to them was the least she could do.

Rex appeared, holding his empty takeout cup, and talking to Jeremy. They were in a deep conversation, giving her a moment to watch him, taking in the line of his jaw, the way his lips moved and his facial expressions. Without the distraction of the blue mohawk, his handsome face was front and centre, and as a woman, she simply had to appreciate it. He was always handsome, with striking blue eyes and a strong, hard jawline, but now he was the definition of sexy. Lost in a daydream, she hadn't noticed that he had turned, and she knew she got caught ogling him instantly, by the boyish smirk on his face. He waved to Jeremy, who leaned over the counter, thanking her for her hospitality as he rushed out the door.

"Can you take a break? Maybe we can go in the back to chat?" Rex asked, gesturing to the back room.

Holly rounded the counter and glanced between them. "I got things covered up here," she said, offering them both a smile.

"Thanks, Holly, I'll be back shortly, but let me know if it gets super busy again, okay?" Harlow insisted.

"Will do!" Holly replied cheerily.

Harlow led Rex to the meeting room in the back and slid the barn door closed, gesturing over to the couch as they both took a seat, on opposite ends, and she said, "So you left me hanging there a bit. What kind of ideas do you have because honestly, I'm willing to do anything right now to keep this business afloat?"

Rex nodded with understanding as he met her curious gaze. "I've been thinking about making some business investments, and I want to invest in Meeting Grounds."

Harlow sat up straighter, not expecting that response, and asked, "Do you mean like a cash investment or partnership?"

"Both actually, but more like a silent partner." He clarified and explained. "Meeting Grounds would remain in your name; no need to change any of the legal stuff, but I would like to get my accountant to look at the books and get some recommendations for improvement. I would also like to infuse some of my cash into this business."

"You can do that?" she asked in surprise.

"The past 5 years have been good to Prairie Sound, and I would like to put some of that money into this community that has always been there for me," he answered, looking around the room. "What you've envisioned and created here, Harlow, is unique and special, and I know it means a lot to a lot of people. So many people depend on the meetings held here, and I want it to be here for years to come. I know I can help you with that," he said, sliding closer and reaching for her hand, lacing his fingers with hers.

She looked down at their joined hands, the way they used to hold hands so many years ago, and unexpected emotion started to well up, making her let out a hiccupped breath as she blinked rapidly, trying desperately to stave off the tears but failing miserably.

"Will you let me help you?" he asked, sliding closer yet, his eyes locked on hers as he brought his other hand up and swiped away tears from her cheeks with his thumb. "I think with my help, you'll be able to have more time with Ty and even be able to take a few days off a week."

A little laugh escaped between her tears, and she let out a long exhale as she replied, "That would be nice."

"Then let's get you a few more staff and in the meantime, I can come in a few days a week." He suggested.

Her eyes darted to meet his gaze with a look of amusement, and she let out a little giggle as she asked, "You want to pour coffee and wipe down tables?"

"Sure, why not?" he replied as he rose from the couch, his hand still holding hers and pulling her up with him. "Right now, we're not touring and still riding out our last album, so I got some time this summer to help you. Besides, don't you think I'll look sexy wearing an apron?" he said with a waggle of his eyebrows.

Harlow blurted out a guffaw and met his gaze, her laughter turning serious as she bridged the gap between them, wrapped her arms around his waist and buried her head in his chest. Hugging him like this — so familiar yet new, masculine scent enveloped her senses as his strong arms came around her and she whispered with a full heart against the comforting warmth of his body, "Thank you."

Rex held her like that for a while, his large hand on her head, holding her to his chest, telling her without words that he was in her corner. In that moment, for the first time in a long time, she felt like everything was going to be okay.

* * *

Pulling up to the two story, modern home in a nice neighbourhood in St. Augustine, Rex grabbed the portfolio he put together for Meeting Grounds and got out of his vehicle. His parents were expecting him for dinner, and he wanted to go through this business plan with his father. Having grown up as the son of a very well known and prolific business owner of Johnson Transport Ltd. he knew his father would appreciate his desire to invest and have some sound advice for him.

"Hey!" he shouted, entering as the smell of slow-cooked meat wafted through the house. Entering the kitchen, his father stood at the long island, dressed in a canvas apron, with a meat fork in one hand and a carving knife in the other, looking like a badass pit boss. "What you got there?" Rex asked, rounding the island.

"Brisket," he replied, slicing a piece off and handing it to Rex. Rex bit into the tender smoked meat and rolled his eyes back. "So good."

"Thanks, son," he replied with a low, deep chuckle as he looked towards the portfolio in his hands. "What have you got there?"

"I'm investing in a business and wanted your opinion." Rex replied, taking a seat on the other side of the island.

"Following the family way." His father mused with an approving nod as he sliced up the meat. "What kind of business are you looking at?"

"It's this new trendy coffee shop on Main Street called Meeting Grounds," he replied. "The premise is that the front of the shop is your standard, trendy, hangout and relaxed-style gourmet coffee shop and in the back, they have a space to host meetings. Specifically, the meeting space is used by the Addictions Foundation. I go there for my SMART Recovery meetings."

"So, you have a personal connection to this business?" he said, nodding his head and meeting his gaze.

"In more ways than one." Rex answered.

"Explain."

"The owner of this business is Harlow Ford." Rex replied.

His dad stopped, looked up at him and put down the knife and fork. "Harlow Ford, like the Harlow you dated in high school. That little blonde firecracker of a girl that was joined to your hip for three years?"

"One and the same." Rex replied. "Only now she is a widowed single Mom, barely keeping her vision for this space afloat and is completely run off her feet."

"How many kids does she have?" he asked curiously.

"One little boy, Tyson. He's five years old."

He nodded and went to the sink to wash his hands as he said, "I always liked Harlow. She had spunk, and she always put you in your place. She was good for you," he said with an amused smile. "Mom and I always wondered what happened there."

"In a nutshell, I was an ass," Rex replied, shaking his head.

"Ah..." his father answered as he rounded the island and came over, reaching for the portfolio, opening it, and reading through the business plan. When he was done, he closed the portfolio, handed it back to Rex and met his gaze. "This looks like it could be a very viable business; she just needs an infusion of cash," he said. "I assume that's how you're investing?"

"Yes, cash and my time. I'll be working there until she can hire and get more staff trained."

"Slinging coffees!" his dad exclaimed, clapping him on the back. "Best way to understand a business is to do the work. Good on you, Rex."

Regardless of his father's thoughts, Rex was invested, both literally and figuratively, but having his father's approval solidified his decision. He was going into business with Harlow.

* * *

"Mommy!" Ty exclaimed as she walked into the family room at her parent's house. He ran towards her, and she picked him up, instantly feeling her back ache with the weight of him.

"You're getting too heavy for Mommy to carry you." She said with a groan as she planted a kiss on his head. "Did you have fun with Granny and Pops?" she asked as her mother came out of the kitchen, a dish towel in hand.

"I did! Pops and I watched baseball and played catch in the backyard." He replied excitedly.

"Well, that sounds fun," she said, as she set him down and took a seat on the opposite end of the couch across from her father and let out a long exhale, her body sore and exhausted.

Her father glanced over and asked, "Long day?" as he returned to flipping through channels.

She nodded, her mother coming into the living room, carrying a plate, and handing it to her with a smile. She glanced down, seeing barbecued chicken, a baked potato fixed just the way she liked it and green salad and looked up at her mother, gratitude in her eyes. "Thanks Mom. I'm famished."

"Eat up, sweetie." She gestured as she took a seat across from them in a large armchair.

Harlow dug in and could feel her mother's eyes on her. "You look tired," she said, her brows furrowed as Ty curled up on her lap, watching the TV. "Are you sleeping okay?"

"Mostly. Just so busy at the shop." She said between bites as she set down her fork and sighed. "Things should get better soon though."

This must have piqued her parent's curiosity as her father muted the TV, and her mother sat up straighter. "I had someone offer to invest in my business, and he wants to hire more staff, so I don't need to be there every day."

"Wow, that's huge. Who's this investor?" her father asked.

"You wouldn't believe it if I told you," she replied, popping a bite of potato into her mouth, chewing, and glancing between them. "It's Rex Johnson."

"T-Rex!" Ty exclaimed from his perch on her mother's lap. "He's my friend."

Her mother frowned, and she gave Harlow a deep look of concern. "Are you taking his help?"

"I am."

"Do you think that's a good idea? I mean, you two have a sordid history, and although I don't know exactly what happened, I know he broke your heart. Plus, didn't he get into some trouble a few years back?" she replied.

"He's a recovering addict." Harlow replied matter-of-factly.

Her mother rolled her eyes. "Honey, seriously, you've been down that road before. Don't get involved in this again." Her mother said, worry in her voice. "I really don't want to see you get hurt."

Harlow shook her head, set down her plate on the coffee table and crossed her arms over her chest, squinting at her mother. "First of all, we're not dating, just friends, and secondly, he's been sober for two years now, has done a long stint in rehab, completed the 12 step program and is currently in SMART Recovery. He is very committed to his sobriety, and he is nothing like he was back in high school."

Her mother gave her a chiding look as she warned, "Be cautious."

Harlow rolled her eyes. "Mom, I'm 30 years old, and both Ty and I have spent some time with him. Trust me when I say this, he's different. The edgy guy you remember is softer now, all edges gone. I wouldn't let Ty be around him if they weren't."

"I personally think if he has even half the business instinct that his father has, having him invest in Meeting Grounds could be a great thing," her father added, glancing back at the TV. "Dale Johnson is far and away one of the savviest business owners in this city."

Harlow turned back to her mother and gave her a look saying, "I know what I'm doing."

Her mother looked away, shook her head, and said, "Just guard your heart, sweetie."

Harlow took in her words, knowing they were ones of

a mother who had picked her shattered daughter off the floor, not once but twice. First with Rex and then with Brendon. Her words were one of a concerned parent, not wanting to see her go through another heartbreak. *Would Rex break my heart again?* Deep down, using her head, not her heart, she knew the answer. *Never.*

CHAPTER 8

The next few weeks were a whirlwind. With a new business plan in place, Rex set in motion a series of events that ensured the longevity of Meeting Grounds. First, he had an inspector come in and check the plumbing and electrical, to ensure there was nothing undisclosed by the holding company that owned the building. And when they found issues, he had his lawyer negotiate with them to get all issues promptly fixed. Then, he put out ads for help, and within three weeks, Harlow had four new employees, and Holly was promoted to shift manager, giving her a raise, and a list of responsibilities that were otherwise on Harlow's plate. Although all the changes were incredible, the best part was the three days a week that Rex came into the shop, apron on and ready to work. The customers loved him, especially the women, and word had gotten out so Prairie Sound fans would come in, gushing when he waited on them.

Harlow would just shake her head and giggle to herself as he charmed and winked his way into filling their tip jar.

He was a natural, and having him around made her feel safe and protected. It gave her a much-needed, long overdue sense of peace.

"Summer in the City is this weekend. Are you ready to be insanely busy?" Rex asked as he mopped the floor and looked up, meeting her gaze.

Harlow let out a long exhale, reaching into the till and taking out the $20 dollar bills to count them. "I think so. I've got the staff now, and we've put together a few specials to draw new customers in. Our regulars seem pretty excited about them too."

He nodded, continuing to mop as she counted the rest of the money in the till, bound it and put it into her bank deposit bag. She leaned on the counter watching him as she often did, her eyes on him being something he thoroughly enjoyed. He knew she was checking him out. She had become obvious with it, and he wasn't about to disappoint her. Returning to the bucket, he dipped the mop in , and pulled it out. He pressed the fibers of the mop, making a show of straining his muscles and making the veins pop out. Stealing a glance at her, she had the corner of her bottom lip between her teeth, and he grinned internally. Harlow always had that tell, even back in high school. "Would you like me to take off my shirt so you can check out the rest of me? I'll gladly give you a show if you want," he teased.

She met his gaze, and released her lip from between her teeth, a rosy hue creeping up her cheeks, as she asked, "Was I that obvious?"

A low chuckle rumbled through his chest as he nodded and he reached over his head, whipping off his shirt, making her breath audibly hitch. "I guess I need to make this one of my duties as assigned." He said with an amused grin.

She picked up a pen and notepad, clicking the pen several times to make a show of it and telling him out loud what she was writing down. "Job description: Topless mopping. Okay, got it down." She said, making him laugh again.

"I'll agree to this duty on one condition." He replied, rubbing his hand along his jaw. "You join me?"

"Topless?" she squeaked out.

"Yeah, you've got a sports bra under there, the blinds are closed and honestly those cover more than a bikini top."

Harlow squinted her eyes at him, as if contemplating his comment, and before he could doubt his brazenness, she whipped off her t-shirt and was standing behind the counter in a black sports bra, her cleavage spilling over the top.

He sucked in a breath, unexpectedly taken aback by the view. *Fuck, she looks good.*

She reached for her pen and notebook and clicked it several times again, her eyes flashing him a naughty look as she deadpanned, "Pants-less dishwashing," and gave him a coy wink.

God, I love this woman.

* * *

PRAIRIE SOUND WAS HEADLINING the Summer in the City concert series, and Harlow was beyond stoked to be able to go see them. Rex had worked his magic, having Holly staff the shop with their new employees so Harlow could have the night off. With Ty partaking in the summer festival with his grandparents, Harlow was free as a bird and, for the first time in a long time, was reminded what it was like to be young and free of any responsibilities. Juli arranged to meet her at the entrance of the park, and she found her there as promised, with Savanah and Emersyn in tow.

The girls hugged her and handed her a backstage pass as they were escorted by security, past the quickly growing crowd to the back of the stage. As they entered the restricted zone, Harlow caught sight of Rex, and she could literally feel the drool pool in her mouth as she took him in. He wore tight, low-slung black jeans that were ripped randomly up to his mid-thigh. Without a shirt on, his taut muscular torso and v-cut at his hips were on full tantalizing display. *Oh, my he looks sexy.* Having noticed a tattoo the other night, she saw it ran along the side of his ribcage, and she could almost make out what it was as they approached. The ladies went to embrace their respective spouses, leaving her standing to the side as Rex swaggered over to her looking positively edible.

"Lost your shirt again." She commented. "Or did you do this for me?" she asked, cocking an eyebrow at him playfully.

"I can neither confirm nor deny," he answered with a waggle of his eyebrows.

"I noticed your tattoo the other night; can I check it out?" she asked as he turned to the side and lifted his arm.

Boldly she ran her hand down his ribcage, his skin

pebbling with goosebumps, as she followed the feathers of what appeared to be a phoenix with her fingertips. Incorporated into the design was a date.

"A phoenix." She observed, admiring the intricate tattoo. "What's this date here?"

He turned to her, his gaze intense as he answered, "The date I almost died."

She removed her fingers and met his intense gaze as she volleyed, "You mean the day you rose from the ashes."

A slow smile curved his lips as the stage director approached them, telling the band it was time to start the show. Rex turned to her, wrapped her up in a hug, the feel of his bare skin and warm tight body against hers, causing an electrical current to charge through her as he planted a kiss on her hair and he said, "Enjoy the show and we'll hang out afterwards, okay?"

She was so taken by the warmth of his embrace and his affectionate gesture that all she could manage to say was, "Yeah, okay," as he followed his bandmates up the stairs to the stage.

The intro to one of their biggest hits started to play, and the crowd went wild as the security guard led them to a special spot just inside the security gate, off to the side.

"Rami requested we have a special place to stand as he's worried about us getting crushed by the crowd." Savanah shouted over the guitar as she ran her hand over her baby bump. "We'll be safe here."

Harlow nodded, although the view wasn't front and centre; from their perch, she had the best view of Rex, and that was all that mattered to her. Thinking back to when they were dating, watching Rex, his intensity behind his drum set, was always something she marvelled at and found a huge turn-on. Now here, over a decade later, his sex appeal seemed to have multiplied tenfold. Gone was the bulky, badass teen with a blue mohawk that first drew her attention, and on stage now was this mature, fit, smoking hot man who was not only a bona fide rockstar but one of the sweetest, kindest, most selfless men she had ever known. And to her above all else, that was sexy as hell. As she watched him play, her pulse surged, her breaths came out laboured, and she knew, in that moment, she was without question, falling for him.

"FUCK, THAT WAS A GREAT CONCERT," Steve said as they exited the stage after their third encore. The chants of the crowd had died down, realizing the concert was now over. "I don't know about you guys, but I always love headlining this festival."

"That's why we do it." Rami said. "St. Augustine, Primrose, all the surrounding communities started us, so it doesn't matter how big we get, we always need to give back to them."

"How much did we raise for the Addictions Foundation tonight?" Rex asked, looking at Layne, who was the treasurer for the Band.

"We sold out, so that's around 5000 tickets, and half the proceeds went to them," he replied. I'll get the number sometime this week.

Rami clapped Rex on the back and smiled, "We did

some good tonight and entertained our fans in the process. Great idea, Rex."

"So, what is everyone doing now?" Layne asked. "Juli and I are kid-free, so we're going to take in the festival."

"Savannah needs her cotton candy." Rami laughed.

"We have plans to check everything out too," Steve replied.

"How about you and Harlow?" Layne asked curiously, his smile growing wider with the question. "Are you two dating now?"

Rex laughed, knowing this question was eventually going to be asked. "No," he replied. "We're just friends."

"For now." Steve added with a smirk. "The chemistry between you two is pretty obvious. Em even asked me what was up."

"There are feelings there." Rex confessed. "Pretty sure she has them too."

"Awesome!" Layne exclaimed. "Juli already has you two married off and having babies."

Rex laughed and replied, "Tell Juli to slow it down; I'm not quite ready for the picket fence yet. I need to fulfill my commitment to this last part of my recovery, and then I'll think about what forever will look like."

"That's smart." Steve replied, knowing how dedicated he was. "You don't want to rush into something before you're ready."

It had been a month since he'd spent the night on her couch, and the stirring of deeper feelings between them became apparent. Although he didn't want them to stop, he also needed to slow himself down a bit. Bide his time. Something as important as his future couldn't be rushed, and he wasn't about to make promises to Harlow and Ty until he fulfilled his promise to himself.

$$* * *$$

MAKING their way through the festival crowd, turning heads, random fans taking pictures, as the band along with their significant others strolled the main street taking in the sights and sounds of the Summer in the City festival. Rex, who had put a shirt on to Harlow's disappointment, walked beside her, his hands in his pockets. She watched his bandmates ahead of them holding their wives' hands, or arms around them lovingly; she felt a little envious. She wanted that, and as she glanced over at Rex casually walking beside her, the urge to reach out and do the same was almost overwhelming. Instead, she looped her arm through his, and he looked down at her, the biggest smile on his face. It was a gesture of a friend, and yet it felt intimate considering their history.

"You were incredible tonight." She said, squeezing his arm. "Every time I see Prairie Sound play, I feel grateful that I got to see where it all began."

"We've come a long way from Layne's garage," he laughed nostalgically. "But I think it's our humble beginnings that keeps us all grounded." His face turned serious, his brows drawing together as he added. "Well, at least now. I kind of became the sex, drugs, and rock n roll cliché."

"You're not now, though." She confirmed, gazing up at him with admiration. "You're one of the kindest, sweetest, most selfless people I know."

He let out a huge guffaw and glanced down at her, meeting her gaze. "Selfless hasn't exactly been my lifetime MO."

"And yet, you are that now," she volleyed back.

He glanced away, swallowing hard, and she felt his body exhale as he turned back to her and said simply. "Thank you."

"I just call it like I see it!" she exclaimed, echoing his words as they bypassed the carnival games and she pulled him towards the bright lights and loud music. "C'mon, Hottie McDrumsticks, you're going to use those big muscles to win me a prize."

"Hottie McDrumsticks?" he asked with a rumbly laugh and an amused smirk.

"Oh, just something Holly and I like to call you behind your back!" she giggled. "Time to use these guns for more than just hitting a drum set."

* * *

THE SUN PEAKED through her curtains, casting shadows on the wall. Harlow slowly opened her eyes, feeling groggy but well-rested. She couldn't remember the last time she didn't need an alarm to get up in the morning. Rolling over, she picked up her phone and glanced at the time. 9:12 a.m. She had slept for over 10 hours and hadn't woken once. She lay back down, staring at the ceiling as she listened for Ty, not a peep coming from his room. Ty was a good sleeper and was always reluctant to wake early with her. Reaching for her phone again, she swiped it open and went to her camera app. Scrolling through pictures from last weekend at the festival, she laughed as she browsed, pictures of the concert, ones she specifically took of Rex in his element, beating on his set, photos of her and the girls, a selfie of her and Juli which she was sure she would print out and put on display somewhere. Perhaps add another photo display to her bedroom wall. She let out a laugh at the ones of Rex giving her goofy faces as he played the carnival games, winning her a stuffed monkey and presenting it to her with a gallant bow before they went to find the rest of their crew. She took in the picture of the group, sitting cozily on the long green couch of her coffee shop, pressed in together as Holly took their picture. Her heart felt full. *These are my friends*. It had been years since she had felt like she was part of something, and with the Prairie Sound crew she felt like she belonged. Lastly, she scrolled to a picture Rex had taken of the two of them, when he grabbed her camera from her hand and told her to smile. Heads bent close, eyes twinkling with mirth, smiles wide and happy. They looked like a couple, and that realization made her heart yearn for that again. Specifically yearn for that with Rex.

As if knowing she was thinking of him, her phone buzzed, a notification from Rex:

The Real Rex Johnson: *I hope I didn't wake you, but I was wondering if you and Ty want to go to the beach today.*

The beach? Harlow sat reading over his invitation again. *It's been years since I have been to a beach. And I've never taken Ty.*

Harlow Ford: *What time? I just woke up.*

The Real Rex Johnson: *Be at your place in an hour and have your bikini ready!*

Dear Lord, I haven't worn a bikini since before having Ty. Harlow rose out of bed and closed her closet door, the full-length mirror appearing, reflecting her image. She lifted her shirt and lowered her sleep shorts, taking in her stomach, which, to her distaste, resembled a deflated balloon. She frowned as she opened her closet and pulled out a bikini she had last worn in her early twenties. She put it back quickly, reaching for a tankini that covered her midriff and sucked in her lower stomach as she threw it on the bed. *No way am I wearing a bikini now.*

An hour later, a knock sounded at her door, and she rushed over to answer it. There leaning against the door-jamb was Rex, dressed in bright blue board shorts with great white sharks in the print, a white tank top that said "beach" across his broad chest and flip-flops. He looked more like a lifeguard than a rock star. Harlow let out a little giggle as she cocked an eyebrow at him. "I swear if you had a buoy under your arm, you could be a lifeguard."

"Too much?" He asked with an amused smirk as he surveyed his beach attire.

"Nope, you'll fit right in!" she replied with another giggle. "Come in. I'm just about to fix some food and drinks to bring along." She said.

"No need to. I got us covered," he replied. "Just you, your bikini and of course, my best bud, Ty!" he said as Ty ran over to him and Rex scooped him up, making him giggle. The sweet sound like music to Harlow's ears.

She grabbed a beach bag, which contained sunscreen, towels and a change of clothes for both her and Ty along with a few other necessities, and was about to sling it over her shoulder when Rex grabbed it. "I got this," he said as he set Ty down and took his hand, flashing her the biggest smile. "Are you two ready for some fun?"

* * *

ARRIVING AT THE BEACH, Rex unloaded his Jeep as Harlow unbuckled a very excited Ty, who was talking a mile a minute. As he removed the cooler and an umbrella, he overheard their conversation.

"Mommy, can I build a sandcastle?" Ty asked.

"We can try, but I don't have any sand toys," she replied, and he glanced up to see her mouth turned into a disappointed frown.

Rex reached for the set of sand toys he had picked up at the store yesterday and came around to the side of the Jeep, holding it up for both Harlow and Ty to see. "Will this work to make that sandcastle?"

"Yes!" Ty exclaimed as he reached for the set and hugged it tightly to his body. "Thank you, T-Rex."

Harlow turned to him, with a grateful gaze mouthing "thank you."

"Told you I had everything covered." he replied with a wink as he turned and reached for the rolling cooler, set a large beach blanket on top and put a long umbrella under his arm before he turned to Harlow and Ty standing beside the Jeep. Harlow let out a giggle and shook her head. "You weren't kidding."

They walked down the path, past the boardwalk until they found a nice part of the beach with clear sand and a little way away from other beachgoers. Rex made quick work of setting everything up as Harlow walked hand in hand with Ty towards the water, and they dipped their toes into the warm lake. Rex looked up from what he was doing, watching them, the scene so beautiful with the shimmering water, blue sky with big fluffy marshmallow clouds and sun bouncing off the golden hue of both Harlow and Ty's blonde hair. He reached into his pocket, took out his phone and snapped a picture to capture the moment. Taking a seat on the blanket, he removed his flip-flops and dug his feet into the warm sand as he watched them, all the while thinking he had never seen anything more perfect. His heart fluttered, a feeling he had never felt before. Harlow turned, her eyes meeting his, the same color as the magnificent sky behind her, and he knew, he knew in that moment, what love was.

HARLOW LIFTED herself off the beach blanket, hearing the giggles of her son, and Rex's deep, bountiful laugh. They had built a masterpiece of a sandcastle, and Rex had surprised Ty by pulling out a bag of mini dinosaurs from a side pocket of his cooler, telling him they needed the dinosaurs to protect the princess that lived in the castle. Ty wholeheartedly agreed, and they had been playing for the past hour, a combination of laughter and dinosaur growls coming from them both. She couldn't help laughing as she watched them play. The scene was so sweet; she had already captured a string of photos to remember it. Rex caught her gaze and rose from the sand, smiling down at Ty affectionately, telling him to stay close as he was going to go talk to his mom. Ty nodded happily, playing as Rex sauntered over, all tanned, shirtless and six-packed with the biggest, cheesiest grin on his face. He took a seat next to Harlow under the umbrella and nudged her shoulder as he said, "Ty is seriously the greatest kid."

"Well, he sure thinks you hung the moon." She replied with a smile. "Thank you for this, by the way; I can't remember the last time I've had this much fun and felt this relaxed."

"Good." he said, removing his sunglasses and meeting her gaze. "You deserve a day like this once in a while."

"I do!" she agreed enthusiastically as she flipped her glasses to the top of her head. Feeling her tankini top rise up, she pulled it down instinctively as she watched Ty play, and her eyes drifted over the beach at all the beautiful women of every size proudly wearing their bikinis looking bold and confident. She was envious of them, of how they just let it all hang out without a care in the world.

"You know, you're the most beautiful woman on this beach, right?" Rex said. Surprised by his comment, she turned and met his insistent gaze. "I mean, I may be a bit biased here, because I've seen you naked before, but seriously, you're still drop-dead sexy."

Harlow blurted out a laugh as she pulled her tankini top down again, covering her midriff. "You need your eyes checked, Rex Johnson."

"Perhaps, you need someone to remind you more often." he volleyed back as his eyes drifted over to her midriff and he commented, "I noticed you're always pulling at your top to cover your stomach, and I keep wondering why? You used to rock a bikini."

"Yeah, well since then I've had a baby, and my stomach resembles a crumpled old parachute. Pregnancy messes your body up." she replied, matter of fact.

"I don't see it." he answered. "I just see a hot mom."

Letting out another guffaw she self consciously pulled at her tankini top. Suddenly his hand covered hers, stopping her, as his large palm slipped under the hem of her top and covered the bare flesh of her stomach. Slowly she turned her head to meet his beautiful blue eyes and swallowed; her mouth suddenly dry as the heat of his hand warmed her belly. "You, Harlow are beautiful and look what your body created and brought into this world." he said gesturing over to Ty happily playing in the sand. "Don't ever put yourself down for that, because in my eyes, you are perfection."

Rex leaned in, and Harlow was sure he was going to kiss her, the moment so raw, honest and intimate. She closed her eyes, bracing for the pillowy softness of his lips, feeling his hot breath on her face and just as she was sure his lips would brush hers; he turned his head and kissed her on the cheek. She let out the breath she'd been holding, and crushing disappointment swelled in her chest. Opening her eyes slowly, she met his gaze as he removed his hand from her belly, the loss of his warmth, adding to the sucker punch of rejection. Feeling emotions rise, she quickly turned away, and put her glasses back on, not wanting him to see how thwarted she suddenly felt. *I need to be alone.* She got up from the blanket and feigned him a smile. "I'm going to cool off in the water. Can you keep an eye on Ty?"

Rex nodded, his brows knit together, and she could feel his eyes bore into her as she walked away.

WATCHING Harlow walk towards the water, he could feel the disappointment radiate off her. He ran his hand over his head and down his face, that whole intimate moment between them surely coming across as a rejection. That was the last thing he wanted her to feel. He wanted to kiss her here on this blanket and nearly did, his inner voice telling him he needed to wait. *Fucking inner voice.* He needed to figure out a way to explain to her how special she was to him, and how much he wanted to be with her without giving her false hope that he would be pursuing her right here right now. *But how do I do that?* He had made a commitment to himself, and he needed to follow it through before he committed to her. He needed to ensure he was in the best possible place so he could be the best possible version of himself for her and Ty. Glancing over to Ty, still playing happily in the sand with his dinosaurs, his heart filled with so much love it almost hurt. The thought of being with Harlow and one day being Ty's dad was something that had started occupying his brain. *Doesn't she see, I want to be a role model for Ty?* He glanced out to the water, seeing Harlow's back turned as she waded into her waist. The desire to run in after her, wrap her up in his arms and kiss her deeply washed over him. But seeing her dejected expression, he knew she needed a moment to be alone to process her feelings. Burgeoning feelings that he felt for her too.

Flipping open the cooler he pulled out a bottle of Coca Cola and twisted off the cap, throwing back a swig of the cold, sugary liquid. He glanced at the bottle, not lost on him, that two and half years ago, it would have been beer filling this cooler instead of soda, water and drink boxes. *You need to wait. Harlow and Ty deserve the best and you can give them that. You just need more time.*

CHAPTER 9

As the summer months grew cold, and school started, Harlow proudly walked her son to the school every morning and waited by the kindergarten door every afternoon. He looked so adorable in his T-Rex backpack which Rex found him. Truth was she was so busy this summer that she hadn't had a chance to find him a backpack and by the time she had a spare moment to look, the selection was meager. Voicing this one day during her shift, apparently gave Rex permission to take charge. Although she would normally tell anyone else to back off, with Rex, she simply couldn't do it. He genuinely cared for them and as the months passed, she could see the love he had for her son. Now if only he had love for her.

Since their beach trip, things had been different between them. They still hung out, both at the coffee shop and on her days off, but after that day something had shifted. Rex would still flirt shamelessly, giving her his best sexy smolder when he got a chance, but she simply couldn't reciprocate. That day on the beach feeling the quell of rejection consume her, it had become apparent to her that she needed to keep him in the friend zone going forward, so she could protect her fragile heart. The problem was she was already gone, feeling feelings for him that were familiar and yet so new. She was falling for him, and to her he had made it clear that it wasn't mutual.

* * *

"It's getting so cold out there." Harlow exclaimed as she looked out at the windy October day. The leaves were swirling around the entrance of the shop and people were walking by, already in winter coats, toques and scarves.

"I always like the cold weather." Holly said as she untied her apron, folded it up and slung it over her arm. "It means snow and snow means snowboarding season is almost here." she said excitedly as she reached for her coat, slipping it on. "Have you ever snowboarded?"

"Nope, and no way are you going to strap a slippery board to my feet and send me down a steep hill." Harlow replied with a laugh. "With my luck I'll hit a tree."

Rex had come through the front door, his jacket collar pulled up over his neck and a beanie on his head. He glanced between Harlow and Holly and raised a brow as he asked, "What are you talking about?"

"Snowboarding!" Holly exclaimed in reply. "Have you been?"

"A few times sure. It's pretty fun." he answered hanging up his coat and putting on his apron.

Holly turned to Harlow a hand on her hip as she said, "See even Rex has tried it."

"You, Harlow, were never much of a thrill seeker." Rex added with a knowing laugh.

She squinted at him, not liking his comment and turned to Holly, "Maybe I'll give snowboarding a try sometime." she replied as her eyes darted to Rex and she raised her chin defiantly. The look on his face was surprised and part of her took perverse satisfaction in that. *Where does he get off acting like he knows everything about me anyways?* She was aware it was silly to be annoyed by him, but she was tired of his comments, claiming he knew her so well. If he knew her as well as he claimed, he could see she was falling for him. She turned away from the conversation, ignored him and gathered some mugs from a table, bringing them to the counter.

Holly said her goodbyes as she slipped out of the front door leaving Harlow and Rex alone.

"Busy today?" he asked, cautiously meeting her gaze then letting his eyes drift over the front of the shop. A few patrons were scattered at tables and the seating areas, visiting, or reading, and drinking their hot beverages to escape the cold outside.

"Yeah, this is the quietest it has been in a while actually." she said not meeting his eyes, but feeling his intense gaze on her and setting to work washing dishes.

"Here, let me do that." he said, sliding in next to her and giving her a wary look. The heat of his body radiated off him and she internally sighed. As much as she was frustrated and hurt by him not wanting her, he was just so darn sweet, it was hard to be angry with him. She let him take over, hearing the bell of the shop ding as one of her regular customers walked in.

"Hey Randy!" she exclaimed in greeting. "It's a blustery one, isn't it?"

"I feel a little like Winnie the Pooh trying to get to his Thoughtful Spot today." he said with a big smile.

Understanding the reference, Harlow giggled and smiled as she fixed him his usual latte. Randy Sherman worked two doors down at the Insurance Agency and was in his mid thirties, tall, lanky, and cute in a very nerdy way. He was very sweet and had an affinity for dad jokes so was always good for a chuckle. Over the summer, Harlow noticed him, going out of his way to simply come chat with her, always ordering his usual latte and lingering as long as possible.

She handed him the latte and he paid her, sensing he was here for more than his favorite drink as he leaned against the coffee bar.

"Harlow, I was wondering if you had plans on Friday night and if not, would you like to have dinner with me?" he asked, a big smile on his questioning face.

Harlow could hear and sense Rex shuffle behind her and something about that miniscule reaction emboldened her. *You may not want me but there is someone that does.* She leaned onto the counter, putting on her full flirt and looking up at Randy through her long lashes.

"I would love to." she answered.

Rex cleared his throat and Randy beamed at her. "Awesome. Can I pick you up here at 6 p.m.?" he asked, taking a sip of his latte, his smile so bright he could stop traffic.

"Sounds great." she replied as Randy made his way to the front door, turned, taking a double take at her and left the building smiling ear to ear.

"A date with Randy, the Insurance guy." Rex said, his voice low and steady. "Not your usual type."

Harlow turned, feeling steam rise to her cheeks. "And you know my type?"

"I think I have a pretty good idea." he volleyed.

"I guess you don't know me as well as you think you do then." she replied pointedly. "Randy is sweet, and kind and he's exactly the kind of guy that won't play around with my heart and emotions. Randy won't lead me on."

Rex held up his hands in surrender, but she could see from his expression her words stung. She could see it in the slump of his shoulders and reflected in the depths of his blue gaze. Although she wasn't one to be mean, something about that look felt satisfying as the phrase *you snooze you lose* floated through her head.

FRIDAY NIGHT, Rex offered to work the late shift so Harlow could go on her date with Randy. Part of him volunteered because he wanted to scope out the situation and make sure Randy was as nice as Harlow said he was. He knew the answer to that even before he asked the question. Randy was a nice guy, always polite, kind to the staff, a little goofy and playful, making everyone laugh, including himself on occasion. Yet the thought of Harlow on a date with him, let alone with another man, was something he wasn't prepared for. He hated that he felt that way, like he had staked a claim on her and no one else could have her. *Why wouldn't they want to be with her?* Harlow was smart, funny, and breathtakingly beautiful. And she was the best mom. She was everything and if he couldn't make her happy, she deserved to find happiness elsewhere even if it made him crazy with jealousy.

Lifting the chairs from the floor and putting them seat down on the tables, he reached for the broom as he swept the floor, the turning leaves being tracked into the shop all day. He was almost done cleaning the floors when in his peripheral vision, he caught a flash of her golden hair, through the picture window at the front of the shop and he leaned against the counter seeing her standing there with Randy. They were facing each other, both talking animatedly with wide smiles on their faces. She threw her head back with a laugh and Randy's face turned serious as he reached out cupping her cheek. She mirrored his expression and Rex knew what was coming. *I can't look,* but his eyes couldn't turn away as Randy lowered his head and brushed his lips to Harlow's. Instantly jealousy bloomed in Rex's chest, an overwhelming desire to be Randy right now, kissing Harlow. His girl, the girl he loved, but couldn't be with yet. *Love?* This was the first time he acknowledged it, the feelings he had for her growing since the day they saw each other again. He rested his elbows on the counter, and gripped his head with his hands, taking deep calming breaths and trying to steady the flood of emotions running through his mind and body. *You're in love with Harlow Ford.* Those words repeated in his mind as he heard the door lock disengage along with the chime and quickly reached for the broom again. He swallowed down hard, in an attempt to push down the emotion and turned to face her, feigning a smile.

"Did you have a good date?" he asked, his words coming out more fractured than he wanted them to.

"I did." she replied, with an apprehensive smile as she took a moment to survey him. "Was everything good here tonight?"

"Fantastic." he squeaked out, internally groaning and chiding himself as he cleared his throat and lowered his voice adding. "Things went well tonight."

"Good." she replied, taking off her coat and setting it over the green couch. "Let me help you clean up."

"No." he replied, quickly meeting her questioning gaze. "You go home and relax, enjoy your night, I got this."

She gave him a wary look, one of both curiosity and concern as she reached for her coat and slipped it back on. "Thanks, Rex." she said quietly. "Have a good night."

He gave her a quick smile as he watched her hesitantly go. Alone he took a seat on his favorite green couch, in the exact spot where he saw again her all those months ago. Hanging his head in defeat, his hands came up covering his face as hot tears stung his eyes and he let a lifetime of regretful emotions out and wept.

* * *

THE NEXT TWO months were some of the longest, Rex could ever remember. Seeing Harlow date, Randy was excruciating and knowing she had introduced him to Ty was enough to completely destroy him. She was moving on from him and finding her happiness and he could do nothing about it. At night when he lay his head down on his pillow, he lay awake for hours thinking about her and wishing she was his. Part of him wondered if all of this was karma. The universe saying, *you hurt her, so you don't deserve to be with her.*

It was mid December; he was seven months into SMART Recovery, past the halfway point and was feeling the home stretch in sight. Five more months and he was done, finally done with his commitment. Although he realistically knew his commitment to sobriety was a life-long one, the fact that he no longer needed to attend meetings and had the tools he needed to stay clean, gave him a peace of mind that he could start to make plans towards his future. Although every time he thought of the future, his plans always included Harlow and Ty.

Harlow walked into the shop, brushing the snow from her coat and feigning him a quick smile as she walked past him into the back storage room. He instantly sensed something was wrong from her clipped expression and glanced over to Holly who had picked up on it too.

"Go ahead." she said, gesturing towards the back room. Rex put down the dish towel he was holding and strode to the back, glancing into her office and not seeing her opening the storage room door.

"Harlow." he called out as he heard a muffled cry and a hiccup from the back corner. Entering the room, he found her facing the shelf of takeout cups, her hands over her face, her shoulders shaking as the unmistakable sound of crying filled the space between them. He approached cautiously and she turned, her face red and streaked with tears as she walked into his embrace and buried her face into his chest. "Harlow, honey, what's wrong?" he asked, his brows furrowed with concern as he stroked her hair to comfort her.

"Randy and I broke up." she managed between hiccups. "He's moving to Florida to be closer to his parents and leaves next week."

"I'm so sorry, Harlow." he said in a soothing tone, despite his self-serving internal voice cheering. "I know you cared about Randy and it's hard when someone you love has to leave."

Harlow stepped out of his embrace, wiping the tears from her face with her palm. "I don't love Randy." she said as she sniffed. "I care about him deeply, and he's the sweetest guy but I know I don't love him."

Rex's brows drew together in confusion as he questioned, "Then why all the tears?"

She started to cry again and looked away for a moment, trying to collect herself as she said, "It was nice to have someone pursue me for a change, you know. Have someone want me." she said as she turned to face him, her red-rimmed eyes firm and resolute. In the depths of her gaze he could see that she was speaking directly to him. "It was nice to not be alone." He stared at her, their eyes locked as his mind screamed, *I'm here! You're not alone. I love you; I want you!* And yet if he said those words now, here in this moment he would just be toying with her heart, and he couldn't hurt her like that. Instead, he wrapped her up in his arms and let her continue to cry all the while thinking, *the next five months are going to be torture.*

With the Christmas rush behind them, things settled down at Meeting Grounds and Harlow was grateful for the quieter days. The regulars still came in along with the odd new patron, escaping the cold Manitoba winter outside. One new patron, a man in his mid twenties, would come in almost daily, ask for a glass of ice water and would find a seat in the corner staring out the front window. He wore a thick wool coat that was a little worse for wear, a slouchy toque over his long blond locks and never took them off. His eyes would dart around the shop and now and then, Harlow would offer him a coffee on the house. He would accept it, not saying anything, just giving her a nod as he sipped it and watched them work. The consensus from her staff was that he was homeless and sought refuge in her shop from the weather outside. Being that her vision for Meeting Grounds was that of a judgement free space she never commented or questioned his presence and left him in peace to simply sit. Besides his presence never raised any concerns for her, he was never rude to the staff or to the other patrons, just faded into the background like the brick wall he sat against. It wasn't until he started taking off his coat, hanging it on the back of his chair and would make his way to the washroom that she and her staff started to feel uneasy. It wasn't the fact that he was using their facilities as it was open to the public, but it was the way he returned, glassy eyed, with a slight but noticeable tremor to his hand. Something about it felt off, like perhaps, he had a condition or was on something. Either way, it was none of their business and since he was never a problem, they didn't have a reason to have a problem with him.

"Wool coat guy here again?" Rex whispered as he glanced towards the corner of the shop, the familiar coat on the back of the chair. The shop was all but empty, just 10 minutes from closing time.

"Yeah. He's in the washroom again, been in there for a while," Harlow replied, a look of concern on her face.

"I'll go knock." Rex offered, striding towards the back, but halfway there the washroom door flew open, and the man's eyes darted away towards where his coat was. Rex gave him a quick smile, but he didn't reciprocate, the man's eyes not meeting his. Something about him looked familiar, like he had seen him before but couldn't pinpoint where exactly. Rex slipped into the washroom, inspecting everything and reaching for the cleaner stored under the sink. He glanced into the garbage can, seeing a substantial amount of toilet paper, red with blood. *Nosebleeds.* He remembered those. That last year when his addiction reached new levels, and he started snorting cocaine. The nosebleeds were constant. Realization what the man had been doing in their washroom, all the signs were there. The glassy eyes and tremors. He had been getting high.

Suddenly a shriek came from outside the washroom, and Rex cautiously opened the door to find the man behind the counter, his arms around Harlow's shoulders, holding something shiny against her neck. *Fuck, it's a knife.*

"Give me everything in the till, or I will cut you," the man warned, loud enough for Rex to hear.

His heart thrumming in his ear, adrenaline kicking in, Rex knew he needed to be cautious. The man was obviously strung out. One jerk of his unsteady hand and he would indeed cut Harlow. He exited the bathroom, walking slowly towards them. The man seeing the movement jerked around to face him, dragging Harlow with him, her face strained in his hold, and Rex met her scared eyes, begging her to remain calm and still.

"I don't want any trouble," the man said, his eyes red-rimmed and cloudy as his hand shook against Harlow's throat. "I just need some money."

Rex slowly pulled his wallet out of his back pocket, lifted it high and showed it to the man. Opening it slowly, he pulled out $500 and held it up. "I have money here for you, but you need to let her go, okay? Put the knife down." Rex could see him loosen his hold, but his shaking hand caused the knife to graze Harlow's neck and nick her, causing a small line of blood to form on her skin. He could see the panic in her eyes as she realized she had been cut, and he willed her not to move as he approached, now mere feet from them. He approached the other side of the counter and laid down the bills, fanning them out so the man could count them. Then he watched as the man jerked his shaking hand away, quickly turned, dropped the knife into the sink with a clink of metal and grabbed the money. Now unarmed, Rex wasn't about to let him get away. The man bolted from behind the coffee bar, rounded the green couch, sprinting for his jacket and Rex cornered him, their eyes locking. Instantly, Rex recognized the man before him as someone he had met in group therapy, his name coming back to him instantly. "Caleb," he said calmly. "You need help."

The man scoffed, seemingly not threatened, slipping on his jacket, his hands shaking as he stuffed the money in his pocket. "You're going to help me?" he questioned with a laugh. "You're just one hit away from where I am right now, Rex."

Rex nodded, knowing he was right, but the difference was that he continued to get help and had the support to overcome his addiction. It was obvious that for Caleb, that wasn't the case. Caleb jerked to the side, trying to foil Rex and escape the shop, but Rex tackled him to the ground, pinning Caleb's arms around his back as he sat on him. He glanced up at Harlow, her face was white as a sheet contrasting against the crimson trails of blood running down her neck, her entire body shaking as she held her phone in her hand, the speaker on as the 911 dispatcher asked, "Is everyone okay?"

"Yes," she croaked out, her voice cracking and high-pitched. "Please come quickly, he's being held down on the ground."

Within minutes, the sound of sirens and the flashing lights of the RCMP pulled up to the front of the building as they entered the coffee shop, surveying the scene. The officers cuffed and arrested Caleb, and Rex sprinted to Harlow's side, surveying the cut on her neck. She reached up with trembling hands and touched the cut, then looked at her hand, now streaked with blood. With that, her eyes rolled back, and he caught her as she passed out in his arms. A female officer came over to help, and as an ambulance pulled up, two paramedics hurried over. He laid her down on the green couch as he stepped back and a medic checked her over. She looked up at Rex and said, "It's just a surface cut, nothing too deep. It doesn't look like it needs stitches. Honestly, it looks worse than it actually is." Rex let out a long exhale, feeling relief washing over him, and he crouched down, brushing her head with affection as the medic continued. "We'll patch her up, and there's no need to bring her in to emergency. Did she pass out from the blood?" she asked. Rex nodded. "That's not uncommon. Probably in shock too. Just give her a few minutes and she'll come to, okay? I'll quickly bandage the wound before she does."

Rex watched as they made short work of disinfecting and sealing the cut as she slowly came to. "Harlow, honey, you're okay," he said as her beautiful blue eyes fluttered open slowly. She jerked up, hand going to her neck, feeling the bandage there.

"Take it easy," the paramedic said, putting her hand on

her shoulder. "You're okay. The cut wasn't deep, and you don't need stitches."

With that, Harlow eased back against the couch, and her eyes darted to Rex as she asked, "Did I faint?"

Nodding, he saw the tears well up in her eyes, and she started to cry. He picked her up and held her on his lap, cradling her as the officers removed the knife, and sat next to them, asking questions as to what happened. Rex answered most of them, Harlow answering what she could through her tears. The female RCMP officer gave her an empathetic look and said, "You're very brave, Ms. Ford."

Ensuring they were fine, the officers exited the shop, and Rex set Harlow down on the couch as he locked the door behind them. Rex reached for her phone and swiped it open. He called her parents and told them what had happened and asked if they could keep Ty for the night, all the while reassuring them that Harlow was safe, and he would stay with her. Then he called Holly, repeated the story and told her not to open tomorrow and to inform the staff. With that, he lifted Harlow up into his arms and carried her out of the building towards his jeep. The silence in the cab was deafening as they drove. He glanced over; her body looked so small and fragile in the seat next to him. Arriving at their destination, Harlow finally broke the silence.

"Where are we?" she croaked out, looking up at his condo building.

"My place." He responded. "You're going to stay with me tonight, okay?"

She nodded and met his gaze. "Ty?"

"He's staying with your parents."

She nodded as he got out of the jeep and opened her door. "Can you walk?" he asked, his brows furrowed in deep concern as he lifted her out of the cab and tried to set her on her feet. She wobbled, falling into his chest, and with that, he lifted her, carrying her into his building, onto the elevator and to his door. Reaching for his keys, he opened his condo door and walked in, immediately heading for his bedroom at the end of the hall. Setting her down on the bed, he walked over to his dresser and pulled out a t-shirt, setting it on the bed next to her. "Do you want my help?" he asked. She didn't respond, just stared forward, her body slumped and looking pale, like she might pass out again or throw up. Undressing her quickly and trying not to take in the creaminess of her skin as he did, he slipped the t-shirt over her head, and pulled back the covers, guiding her into his bed. She immediately curled into a ball and closed her eyes. He crouched down, tucking a strand of her golden locks behind her ear and leaned in, kissing her forehead. Her eyes fluttered, but otherwise she didn't stir. The crash of the adrenaline high was obviously exhausting her and making her fall into a deep sleep. Rising to his feet, he could feel the ache in his entire upper body, as the adrenaline of what happened tonight, left him too. Feeling exhausted, all he wanted to do was lie next to her, to protect her. He pulled off his shirt and jeans, throwing them into a hamper, and pulled out a pair of sleep pants from a drawer, slipping them on. Rounding to the other side of the bed, he slid in next to her, feeling the warmth of her body beside him. Wanting to envelop her in his protection, he curled up around her, pulling her body into his and burying his face in her soft hair. "You're safe," he whispered as he closed his eyes and drifted off to sleep.

* * *

THE NEXT MORNING, Rex woke from a most amazing dream. He was kissing the side of Harlow's neck, feeling the silky softness of her skin on his lips. She moaned, a long-drawn-out moan that made him instantly hard and ready for her. His hand slid over the curve of her hip and up her side, grazing the underside of her breast when he heard her say his name in a breathy voice, "Rex."

Her voice was so clear, like it was in the room and not part of his dream. Suddenly he realized it wasn't a dream at all. He was grinding himself against her behind, and his hand was up the t-shirt, nearly caressing her breast. He pulled away, frustrated with himself and instantly feeling ashamed. *Rex, you idiot.*

"Why'd you stop?" she breathed out, turning to look at him over her shoulder.

"We can't." he replied simply as he lay on his back staring up at the ceiling.

"Why not?" She asked as she turned fully to face him, shifted her body and climbed on top of him, straddling his hips. The heat of her core made him grow impossibly harder as she leaned forward mere inches from his lips, her blue eyes dark with desire. "I want you to kiss me."

"I can't," he pleaded, his resolve teetering as she lowered her lips so close to his that they were sharing the same breath.

"I need you to kiss me, Rex. I need you to touch me," she begged as she put his hands on her behind and moved above him, rubbing her core over the hardness in his sleep pants.

He groaned, feeling his willpower slip through his fingers as she leaned forward again to capture his lips, and he turned quickly, her lips brushing his cheek.

She pulled away, sitting up straight, her eyes blazing as fiery red rose on her cheeks. "You make no sense, Rex Johnson," she said with frustration edging her voice. "You flirt with me, you tell me I'm so beautiful, you make me feel special. You look at me constantly like you want to kiss me, you save my business, you protect me, hold me all night long and make me feel safe. You love my kid, like he's yours. And you refuse to make love to me. You refuse to touch me."

"Harlow, I..." he began, begging her with his eyes to understand.

"No!" she shouted, crawling off him and reaching for her jeans he had set on the dresser. "You can't play with my emotions like that. Be all sweet to me and give me false hope that you and I could work out and have our happily ever after. You can't let me fall in love with you and then deny me all of you. I won't let you hurt me again, Rex. Not like this, because this is so much worse than when you cheated on me. This rejection now is like a stab to the heart." She croaked out her fist hitting her chest.

"Harlow, please stop. I can explain, just..."

"No!" she shouted again. "You're not allowed to break my heart again. You're not allowed to make me feel unwanted," she said, whipping off his shirt and putting hers back on in a frenzy as she stomped down his hallway towards the front door looking for her coat and shoes.

"Honey, you need to stop; it's not like that," he begged as he followed her.

She turned to him, flames shooting from her eyes. "What is it then, Rex? Am I not sexy enough for you? Not the cute little blonde that hung onto every morsel of affection you threw her way anymore. Am I too battered and bruised now? Carry too much baggage and hurt at the way her life turned out. Am I not enough?"

Rex stared at her, feeling every insecurity she was voicing and wanting to take them all away.

"You are more than enough for me," he breathed out.

She huffed and picked up a shoe, sliding it on. "Then why won't you fucking touch me!" she yelled out as exasperated tears formed in her eyes. She blinked, and her shoulders started to shake as she started to cry out of anger, disappointment and frustration.

"Harlow, stop, just stop," he said, his hand now on her waist as he pressed her to the door and caged her in with his other arm. "Honey, just stop."

Letting out an exasperated huff, her eyes met his. He could feel the heat coming from her face, a scorching burn sizzling from the tears on her cheeks.

"Stop," he whispered in a soothing tone. "Please don't be angry."

"I'm not angry, well yes, I'm angry, but I'm more frustrated, so sexually frustrated that you won't give me this. That you don't desire me as much as I desire you." She breathed out, her chest heaving with each word as she matched his intense gaze. "Why don't you want me?"

"Do you honestly think that I don't want you?" he asked, his brows furrowed but his eyes still locked on hers.

"Yes," she answered, putting her chin out defiantly. "That's why you won't kiss me, put your hands on my body and fuck me."

He pressed his hard, taut body into hers, the burning heat of him making her breath hitch as his jaw locked with restraint. His ironclad willpower barely hanging on as he spoke in a low, controlled voice. "It would be so easy, Harlow, to lift you and fuck you right here against this door. To bury myself in your gorgeous body and make you scream my name as I take you hard and dirty." He could feel her body tremble at his words. A frenzied desire threatened to escape as his eyes searched hers. "My desire for you literally burns me from the inside out, Harlow. I feel it in my bones; that's how much I want you. It's like an electrical current that surges through me every time I'm with you. You, Harlow, consume me in a way I never thought I could be consumed." He said, his hand sliding into her hair as his fingertips tenderly massaged her scalp and his face lowered, a mere inch from hers. The tip of his tongue darted out, and he licked his bottom lip, her eyes following his movement. "I've wanted to kiss you senseless. To touch your beautiful body. To taste every inch of your skin from the moment I saw you. It has taken everything inside of me to resist the urge to take you. I knew if I gave in and took what I wanted, you would get hurt."

"Rex, I won't get hurt, I won't, I know myself," she begged, her hands running up the side of his torso, making him close his eyes and hiss through his teeth. "I need you."

He took a deep breath, his eyes opening slowly, conviction in their depths as he continued. "I need you to be patient, Harlow. I need you to understand that my turning you down and not giving in today is what's best for me and for you and, most importantly, for Ty. I need to complete my sobriety commitment before I commit to you. And Harlow, that's exactly what it's going to be. A commitment. I want you and Ty in my life forever and want you two to be my future. Don't you see? That's how serious I am, honey."

Rex felt her body soften with his words, knowing she wanted that more than anything too. He couldn't imagine Harlow and Ty not being a permanent part of his life now, and the thought of spending his lifetime with them filled him with a rush of happiness and contentment that he was sure he could never find elsewhere.

"We are just on the edge of forever, Harlow. I need you to be patient. In three months, I'll be done with SMART Recovery, and then I want to kiss you, touch you and make love to you the way you deserve to be loved. I want you to know, beyond a shadow of a doubt, that I am 100% yours and that my past addiction will never be a part of our narrative going forward," he said, his forehead meeting hers, their eyes locked. "And that's what it's going to be for me, Harlow, my love. That's what I feel for you. But I won't say those three words until I've done what I need to do, to be the best version of myself for you and Ty."

"Three months?" She asked with a deep sigh.

"Three months." he answered.

Harlow looked down, her gaze roaming over his torso and drifting back to his eyes so full of love and desire for him. She swallowed down the last bit of her frustration and replied, "Then let me mark my calendar."

CHAPTER 11

For three months, Rex, Harlow and Ty spent as much time together as they could. As an outsider looking in, one would have thought they were a family, but behind closed doors, Rex kept his promise to himself and to her. They held hands, cuddled, and some nights held each other, but they never kissed and were never intimate. The last three months of his recovery felt like a time of renewal for him and for them. Like a time that righted the wrongs of the past and allowed them to hit a reset button on their relationship. This time, making them a stronger unit for their promised future.

"Two weeks." Harlow said, wrapping her arms around his waist and resting her cheek on his back affectionately.

"Two weeks." He replied, flipping some pancakes on a griddle as Ty watched him from his perch at his island. "Blueberries or chocolate chips, Ty."

"Both!" he exclaimed. Rex gave him a wink as he added both to his pancakes. Almost done with kindergarten, Ty had gone from a quiet, super soft-spoken kid to confident and outgoing, having found his voice and social footing.

Rex loved these lazy Sunday mornings when they spent the night at his place, sleeping in, making a leisurely breakfast, and watching cartoons or movies together. It was simple and beautiful, and the more Sundays they spent like this together, the more days he wanted. He wanted his space to be their space, and that was something he needed to discuss with Harlow sooner rather than later. Placing Ty's pancakes on his plate, Harlow came around and cut them for Ty, pouring Syrup in a little container on the side so he could dip the pieces as he liked.

"Can I eat in the living room and watch cartoons?" Ty asked, picking up his plate.

"Sure, buddy." Rex replied with a smile as he hopped off the stool, nearly dumping his container of syrup. Harlow winced, and Ty turned with a big grin on his face, giving them a thumbs up. Rex just shook his head and laughed as he turned to face Harlow, his hands on her waist. He lowered his head, their foreheads meeting as their eyes locked on each other.

"It's hard to believe how fast these past few months have gone." She said with a sigh.

"Not fast enough." He replied, breathing in deeply as he pulled her a little closer. "I'm dying to kiss you."

"You could now; I won't tell anyone." She replied playfully.

"I don't think we could keep it PG if we started though." He replied, glancing behind them at Ty.

"Agreed, we would definitely need one of those

disclaimers before a TV show or movie that says, May contain sexually explicit scenes and nudity." She deadpanned.

He threw his head back in a laugh and wrapped his arms around her, loving how she fit so perfectly in his embrace, and kissed her head affectionately. As he held her, the weight of what was coming for them and how important it was to Harlow overwhelmed him. Although he wanted her with every fiber of his being, he had this little voice of insecurity that kept planting seeds of doubt in his head. He couldn't remember having sex sober. Over a decade of sexual experiences, either drunk or high. *Will I be good at it? Will I be able to satisfy her? Do I even know what I'm doing?* He had read up on how sobriety and sex related and how, for some, it messed up their libidos, affecting their relationships. *Would that be a challenge they had to face?* He didn't have answers, but he knew who he could be candid with - *Jeremy.*

REX WALKED into the gym and immediately spotted Jeremy sparring with someone in the boxing ring. He walked over and shouted, "Weak punches, old man?"

Jeremy pulled off his gloves and shook his sparring partner's hand as he exited the ring. Removing his mouth guard and helmet, he gestured to the bench for them to take a seat.

"I always know if you show up here, not on a workout day, you're here to talk," he said. "So, what do you have for me today?"

"I got two more weeks of SMART Recovery as you know..." Rex started.

"On the home stretch." Jeremy said, clapping him on the back. "Well done."

"And as you know, I've been holding out on a relationship with Harlow until the program is complete." Rex added. Jeremy nodded, remembering their conversation. "Harlow and I have built up this moment where we can finally be together, and I'm not sure if I know how to love her the way she wants me to love her...sober." Rex confessed, meeting his gaze.

"Do you mean you're not sure if you can rise to the occasion?" He asked, seriousness in his tone.

"Oh, I'm sure I can rise to the occasion; that part has been proven. It's just I've never had sex sober, and any sex I had prior to my addiction was that of a sloppy, horny teenager." He replied, running his hand over his short hair. "I'm scared of disappointing her."

"Have you told her this?" Jeremy asked.

"No," Rex replied. "But I know she's expecting fireworks, and I'm afraid all I'll bring to the party is a sparkler."

Jeremy let out a bountiful laugh and nodded his head in approval as he said, "Great analogy!"

"Seriously, though, what if I can't perform to her expectations?" Rex asked, furrowing his brows.

"It's a valid concern." Jeremy replied, giving his shoulder a squeeze. "You've always associated sex with drugs, and now, sober sex to you means intimacy with someone you love."

"Exactly."

"Honestly, I think that your concerns and anxieties around it are valid, but if she loves you as much as you love her, she'll be patient with you."

"Do you think?" Rex asked.

"I know. But you need to talk to her about it. Manage her expectations and then in two weeks, feel it out. Pun intended," he said with a waggle of his brows.

Rex laughed and gave him a grateful look. Jeremy was right; he needed to talk to Harlow and put everything out on the table. If he was going to be with her, she needed to know how he was feeling before they took that next step.

A COUPLE of fans came into Meeting Grounds, immediately taking a seat where they knew Rex would be serving them. They giggled as he joked and flirted with them, autographed their cups of coffee, and took selfies. Harlow didn't mind; in fact, she was so used to it, she found it sweet how he showered his fans with attention. Everything about it was innocent and made his fans happy. He walked over to the coffee counter as she leaned on it and met his gaze.

"Part of your fan club?" she asked, a smile tugging at her lips as she glanced at the clock on the wall. "5 minutes until closing time." She said, leaning back to stretch and letting out a tired sigh.

The gaggle of female fans waved over to Rex, and he exclaimed, "Come again, ladies!" as they exited the shop. With no other patrons left, Rex walked over to the front door, flipped the sign to closed and engaged the lock. He turned to her, approaching slowly, with a serious look on his face.

"Harlow, do you have a few minutes to chat before we do the end of day clean up?" he asked, gesturing over to their favorite green couch.

Harlow nodded, a hesitant look on her face, as she rounded the couch and took a seat across from him, reaching for his hands and threading her fingers through his.

Feeling the anxiety of this conversation thrum through him, he took a long breath and blurted out, "I've never had sex sober."

Harlow let out an inadvertent "oh," straightened her back and met his gaze, her brows furrowing. "Most of the times we were together, at least at the beginning, you hadn't been drinking or getting high."

"Yeah, but it wasn't like I knew what I was doing back then. We were more concerned about getting caught, so everything we did was quick and dirty," he replied.

She let out a little laugh. "We never did get caught though."

A smile tugged at his lips at the memories, but it quickly morphed into seriousness. "For me, the parts of my sexual experiences I can remember were those of someone singularly focused. I was a man who wanted to get off, rather than make whomever I was sleeping with feel good," he explained. "Sex was part of the buzz."

"And you're worried you won't satisfy me?" she asked, moving closer and glancing at their joined hands.

"Yeah," he answered. "We've waited so long to be together that I'm scared I won't meet your expectations."

Harlow was quiet for a moment, then let go of his hands and rose from the couch. She climbed onto his lap, straddling his hips, and took his face in her hands. Staring deep into his eyes, she said, "Rex you've already met and surpassed any expectation I have of you and when we can finally be together and make love, our incredible connection and love for each other is what's going to make it amazing. And if we stumble a little, we'll figure it out together."

Rex searched her eyes, seeing only love, honesty and devotion in their depths. *How did I ever get so lucky?* She hooked her arms around his waist and rested her head in the crook of his neck, her warm breath comforting against his skin. His arms came around her, and he smiled a reassured smile as her words echoed in his head and his heart swelled with love for this woman. *We'll figure it out together.*

To say the two weeks until Rex was done with his recovery took forever was the understatement of the century. The days dragged by slowly, first one meeting and then today the last one. It was time for their next chapter to begin, and this time it would be together. After Rex's confession, Harlow had given a lot of thought to how she wanted their first night together to go. Part of her wanted to set up something cheesy and romantic and go a little over the top, but in the end nothing she could plan would seem as important as actually being together.

The barn door slid open from the back room and Rex

walked out, his grin that of a man proud of what he had accomplished. Harlow rounded the coffee bar and met him, his eyes dancing. He glanced around her and shouted over to Holly, "Can you find someone to cover for Harlow? She's going to be very busy for the next few days."

"I think so!" she shouted back, looking between the two of them with a knowing smirk on her face.

His eyes returned to hers, intense, and dark. "Good," he said, pulling her flush with his hard body and making her let out a little squeal as he leaned into her ear and whispered, "Because I need to make love to my girlfriend."

Shivers ran down her spine as he picked her up and threw her over his shoulder, making her squeal again and start giggling. The patrons taking in the scene clapped, Holly whistled and cheered, and Jeremy let out a huge, bountiful laugh as he clapped Rex on the back. "Have fun you crazy kids."

With that, Rex carried Harlow out of Meeting Grounds caveman style, patrons and pedestrians turning their attention to them as he set her down next to his Jeep and opened the door to let her climb in. The drive to his condo was a quick one, both breathing hard with anticipation as he parked and came around to open her door. She gave him a coquettish grin and bit her bottom lip, looking up at him, her eyes willing him to kiss her. "Kiss me," she breathed out.

He pulled her flush with his body and sucked in his breath with his teeth as he replied, "Harlow I'm all for PDA, but if we start here in the parking lot, we're going to give the neighbours a show as I'm not going to stop."

She giggled as she replied, "Okay, okay, I get it, no peep show for the neighbours."

He laughed, took her hand and they entered the building, boarding the elevator, the sexual tension between them ready to combust as their eyes watched the floors go up excruciatingly slow. The door opened, both of their breaths laboured as they walked down the hall to his condo door, and he pulled out the keys, his eyes meeting hers. Rex paused a beat, as if trying to memorize this moment, the moment before everything was about to change.

OPENING THE DOOR, Harlow walked in, Rex following behind. Flipping the lock, he turned to her; the heat radiating between them like a fire ready to ignite. Wasting no time bridging the gap, he lifted her into his arms, and she wrapped her legs around him, looping her arms around his neck. He carried her to the island and set her down on the counter. The look on her face was that of someone so hopelessly in love, and he knew right then and there, he needed to say those magical words he held back for this moment, and she so desperately wanted to hear.

"I love you, Harlow," he said, the emotion making his voice break.

Her eyes welled up, and she closed them, letting out a long breath as she whispered. "Say it again."

"I love you. I love you so much, Harlow. You are it for me."

Tears escaped through her lashes, and he kissed one

side and then the other, the saltiness of her happy tears, like a promise. She opened her eyes, his lips a breath away from hers as they took in the same air.

"I love you too," she breathed out, as he captured her lips and stole her breath, kissing her hard and deep, revelling in the feel of her soft lips against his own. He had kissed more than his share of women. Each kiss a means to an end and in a haze of booze and drugs. With Harlow now, their lips hungry and wanton, needing to be quenched by each other, this felt like it was the first true kiss of his life. A kiss that would remain burned in his brain and branded on his heart. She moaned against his lips, parting them slightly to invite him in. Their tongues tasting and exploring, a preview of what was yet to come.

Harlow pulled her lips away, hazy with lust as her chest heaved with each word from her mouth. "Make love to me, Rex."

With her words, he lifted her from the counter as they continued to kiss, carrying her to his bedroom. Setting her beside his bed, he cupped her cheek, caressing the tender skin as she kissed his palm and looked up at him, her eyes reflecting lust and love. He reached over his head, pulling off his t-shirt and reaching for the hem of her t-shirt. He lifted it slowly, as he watched each inch of creamy skin be revealed. She lifted her arms as he pulled it over her head and shook out her golden blonde locks. Rex's eyes roamed over her, marveling at how breath-taking she looked standing before him, in a black lace bra, barely covering her ample breasts, pert and peaked. She ran her hands up his stomach and leaned in, kissing each ab that her fingertips traced. He watched her, his breathing heavy, his arousal pressing hard against his jeans. Her hands roamed each groove and edge of his upper body. As her hand trailed to the button of his jeans, she looked up, her lustful gaze meeting his while she popped the button and slid the zipper down. With a shaking hand, he reached for the button of her jeans, and she took over, her eyes locked on his as she slowly removed her jeans, leaving her in a pair of black lace bikini panties. She instinctively covered her lower stomach with her hand. Gently, he pulled it away and took in the sight of her before their eyes met with intensity.

"You are the most beautiful woman I have ever seen."

Her breath hitched with his words as he slowly removed his jeans, leaving him in his boxer briefs before her. She backed him towards the bed, letting him fall onto the mattress, and crawled over him to straddle his hips, the heat of her core flush with the hard ridge barely restrained by his briefs. She looked down at him, her blue eyes dreamy as she leaned in, kissing him sensually, dipping her tongue into his mouth and tangling with his. Pulling her lips away, she rocked above him, rubbing against his ridge as she reached behind her back, unfastening the clasp of her bra, freeing her breasts. Her body was no longer that of a teenager but of a mature, beautiful, and bold woman. Stilling, she let him take his fill of her, his eyes wandering over her full, pert breasts, wanting to memorize every swell and curve. His gaze rose back to hers as he pulled her into his body and rolled them, her underneath with him pressing her into the mattress, caging her in with his arms. Her breasts heaved against his chest, their peaks diamond hard as they brushed his skin, and she said breathlessly, "I want you so much, I don't know where to begin."

"There's something you and I have never done." He answered, his mouth salivating at the thought. Her eyebrows raised in curiosity as she asked, "Hadn't we done pretty much everything?" He shook his head and met her gaze, his eyes dark with desire, "I've never gone down on you."

She sucked in a breath as he leaned in kissing her lips hungrily, his mouth roaming as he branded hot kisses along her jaw and down her neck, kissing each shoulder and trailing his tongue down the middle of her breasts cupping one, teasing the peak with his thumb then with his tongue pulling at the taut peak with his teeth before releasing it, making her moan. He kissed his way to the other side, giving the other breast his attention before he trailed his tongue down her stomach, stopping where he knew she was self-conscious. Hooking his fingers into the sides of her panties, drawing them down and revealing her fully to him, he raised his head, meeting her eyes as he lowered his lips and kissed the place where she carried Ty, letting her know he loved every inch of her womanly body just as it was.

* * *

HARLOW'S BRAIN WAS SHORT-CIRCUITING, Rex's slow and sensual taunt making her ridiculously aroused. It had never been like this between them. Sex satisfying but always frantic, hard and fast. He was savoring her, relishing her body, reading her cues and giving her what she wanted. What she needed. It was a slow burn, like their rekindled relationship, taking their time so they could get it right. There would be time for crazy, animalistic sex later; right now, it was all about drawing out this precious moment in time and showing how much they loved each other.

Letting her legs fall to the side, he kissed the juncture of her core and slid his tongue between her folds, finding the most sensitive part of her, that if given his attention could make her lose control. He teased, his tongue sliding along her seam as he lapped at her, long lavished licks where she needed it most. She closed her eyes, moaning, writhing, and unapologetically rocking against his mouth all the while thinking how sex had never felt this impossibly good. "Oh God, Rex, I'm going to come!" she cried out, feeling that burn of pleasure crest as she cried out. "Rex!"

He didn't relent, devouring her core as she rode out her orgasm and with a sigh trembled as he looked up, the most satisfied grin on his face. She giggled and breathed heavily as he climbed off the bed and curled his fingers around the waistband of his briefs, pulling them down, baring himself to her. She rose on her elbows, her eyes roaming over his taut body and settling on the hard steel length of him, which was so much better than she remembered. Rex climbed back onto the bed, nestling between her legs, then hesitated. "Shit, I need to grab a condom," he said as he rose to climb off the bed again.

Pulling him back down on top of her and she shook

her head. "I don't want anything between us. I'm clean, are you?"

"Yes, I've been tested." He replied, cupping her head between his hands as he hovered above her, searching her eyes. "Are you sure? You could get pregnant."

"Then I get pregnant. I am pretty sure I want to have like a dozen babies with you, Rex Johnson," she replied with a little giggle.

A smile tugged at his lips with her words as he replied. "I want to have a family with you too, Harlow."

"Then make love to me and let fate take its course." She replied, running her hand over his back lovingly.

With eyes locked on the future, he pressed himself into her slowly, filling her inch by glorious inch, the feel of him so perfect it made her eyes flutter at the fullness. She met his gaze, a man so in awe and reverent, it made tears threaten to escape. No one had ever looked at her like that. Like she was his past, his present and his future.

"I love you, Harlow," he said, his voice strained with emotion and wanton desire.

"I love you too," she replied, capturing his lips as he set a steady rhythm, meeting each grind and press with her own. Each as sweet and perfect as the next.

"You feel so fucking good," he groaned out as he pulled her leg up, hitching it high to deepen the angle and making her moan out with unbridled pleasure.

She could feel that tantalizing sizzle deep in her core, her body begging for release as he drew out her pleasure slowly and sensually until she was sure she couldn't take it anymore.

* * *

THIS IS what sober sex feels like? His mind a haze of lust and love as he moved inside Harlow, her body, drawing him in, deeper with each thrust of his hips. He could feel her inner muscles pulsate and ripple over him, his senses heightened with all these new sensations, and he sensed she was close. The sweet burn had been moving slowly up his spine, building at a steady pace, knowing he couldn't hold back any longer.

"I'm so close, honey, please tell me you're there too," he managed to breathe out.

With his words, she gasped, her inner muscles tightened like a vice grip, sparking his body to action. With one, two, three more delicious slides, he was there with her, their writhing bodies shuddering with pleasure as they tumbled together into pure ecstasy. And that was exactly what it felt like, complete ecstasy. Better than any drug, the high of making love to the woman he planned on spending the rest of his life with was more powerful and potent than any substance.

He collapsed on her, his body still buried deep in hers as they lay there, their skin wet with sweat, their bodies spent from exertion. Not wanting to crush her, he rolled to the side and turned his head to look over at her, her chest heaving as she tried to catch her breath. Harlow slowly turned her head to face him, her eyes lustful and dreamy as she said, "So worth the wait."

CHAPTER 12

"Are we ever going to leave this bed?" Harlow asked with a giggle as she traced figure eights on his chest.

"Not for two days at least," he replied. "Your mom took Ty till Sunday night, and I plan on keeping you naked until then."

The sun had gone down, neither having left the bed for more than a glass of water or a quick trip to the bathroom since noon. "What if I told you I'm getting hungry?" she asked, running her hands over the washboard of his abs. "A girl cannot live on great sex alone."

He laughed and captured her lips, chaste and hungry, then climbed out of bed, her eyes watching his naked body as she bit her bottom lip, giving him a look of approval at what she saw. Reaching down where he had discarded his jeans, he dug into his pocket to retrieve his phone and brought it back to the bed. Looking at her, he asked, "What do you want?"

"Do you think Sal's delivers?"

"Poutine?" he asked with a smile.

She nodded emphatically.

"I've never eaten Poutine naked before," he replied with a waggle of his eyebrows. "So many firsts today." He added as he looked on their website, noticing he could get them delivered through an app. Within a few minutes their dinner was ordered, and Harlow was straddling his lap, his hands coasting over her curves, his eyes locked on hers.

"Is there anything else you haven't done and want to try?" she asked, sliding her hands over his chest and stomach.

"Honestly, I feel like everything. I don't remember most of my sexual experiences, Harlow. They are a haze to me. All faded by drugs and alcohol. The only times I truly remember are the ones you and I experienced together in our first two years," he answered truthfully.

"So, you were high that last year?" She asked, her gaze languidly meeting his, with no judgement in her question.

"Pretty much." He replied with gritted teeth. "It's no excuse, but I think it numbed my feelings for anything that mattered to me. And that included you," he replied, glancing away to sort his thoughts and words, then turning his gaze back to her. "I'm so sorry I hurt you like that. I cared so deeply for you, but I would be lying if I said I loved you back then. I don't think I was capable of loving anyone at that time, including myself. And I took advantage of your affections as I knew beyond a shadow of a doubt that you loved me."

"I was mad about you back then..." she started, her voice lowering. "...until I was mad at you."

Rex swallowed, feeling the shame rise in his chest, the emotion of what he did to her, how he betrayed her trust resurfacing and making him wish he could erase the past.

"But I don't think we would have worked out back then, regardless." She added, meeting his gaze. "We were so young, and I know you say you were immature, but I was too. I had no idea what I wanted out of life back then. I lived and breathed for you; that was it. But you breaking my heart made me start to live and breathe for myself, and if I hadn't endured that heartbreak I wouldn't have gone on with my life, finished college, married Brendon and had Ty. I wouldn't have moved back to St. Augustine and opened Meeting Grounds. I wouldn't have reconnected with you. Don't you see? We needed to go through the painful parts to get to the good stuff. To truly appreciate each other. I truly believe we were always destined to be together, Rex, but we just need to be in the right place in our lives to recognize it. Now we're ready to fulfill that destiny."

He absorbed her words, a knowing smile curving his lips as he asked, "How did I get so lucky? A woman both sexy and smart. I am the luckiest man in the world."

"You are," she replied with a sassy wink as she lowered her lips to his, kissing him gently yet passionately as she rocked against him and stirred him to life. Just then, a knock sounded at the door, making Rex groan as he sucked in a breath between his teeth. "Our food." She replied, getting off him and pulling the blanket over her.

He got out of bed and clumsily wrestled himself into his jeans, making Harlow laugh as he waggled his eyebrows at her. "Be right back."

Harlow crawled out of the bed, reaching for his t-shirt on the ground and slipping it on. The shirt just covered her as she walked toward the kitchen. Rex had just closed the door and turned into the kitchen when he saw her.

"You're dressed?" he asked, holding the takeout bag.

"Technically, but very naked under your t-shirt," she said, giving him a sexy grin.

He laughed, opening the takeout bag and handing her a container. Taking a seat at the island, she went through her ritual, smelling the poutine first and then taking that first bite. Savoring the rich gravy, salty cheese and crispy homemade fries. She groaned and rolled her eyes in approval as she devoured her meal. She looked up, reached for a napkin to dab her mouth and smiled seeing Rex leaning on the island watching her.

"I think I could watch you eat poutine for the rest of my life," he said.

Narrowing her eyes, she scrutinized him a moment, a question floating through her head that needed to be asked. "I know you've said you see us being together forever, but what does that look like for you?"

Rex took in her question and composed his answer - one that would clarify his intentions and what he saw for their future. He rounded the island, settling on the stool next to her. Taking her hands in his, he stared at their hands for a moment, and his eyes drifted up to hers, so much love and sincerity enveloping her. "I see us getting married, you and Ty moving in here until we can find a house, and us starting a family together."

Sighing, she replied, "That's what I want too."

"And I see myself adopting Ty," he added. "I'll always

want to keep Brendon's memory alive for Ty, but I want to be his father and for him to carry my name. Would you be okay with that?"

Harlow looked down at their fingers now laced together, a solid mass of skin and bone, hardly distinguishable between her fingers and his. Something about the unity it represented made her answer to him so easy. From the day Rex walked back into their life again, and from the first loving look he gave her son, she knew that Rex was the father that her son not only needed but deserved. He had proven his devotion and love for her son, and she wanted nothing more for them to be a family.

"I would love for you to be Ty's father." She said, her voice cracking with emotion as a tear escaped through her lashes, rolling down her cheek.

He reached out and captured it with his thumb, caressing her cheek with affection as he said, "I know this isn't super romantic, but I can't wait any longer." he said, releasing their intertwined hands and getting up from the stool. "Be right back."

Harlow watched him disappear down the hall, confused but curious. He reappeared a minute later, with something in his hand. He took a seat across from her again and took her left hand in his, looking down at it with reverence as his eyes drifted back to hers. "Harlow, I want to give you and Ty a beautiful life, full of happiness and love, and even if we waited, my desire to give that to you both would not change. I know what I want, and I want you. Will you be my wife and marry me?"

Harlow brought her other hand to her chest, holding it

over her heart as he opened his palm to reveal a stunning gold ring with the most gorgeous blue stone she had ever seen. He held it up; the light glinting on the cut of the stone, making it shimmer. "I was in Europe on tour with the band about six years ago, and we were in Hamburg at the time. Layne had just reunited with Juli and Steve, and Rami were still sleeping. I was hungover, but in a rare moment of sobriety, I couldn't sleep, so I went for a walk." He swallowed hard as he continued. "At the time, I knew I was spiraling. My days were concerts and booze, plus I had experimented with hard drugs. My life wasn't my own, and I was losing control. As I walked down the street, I took in some of the shops along the promenade and noticed this little precious gem shop with this ring in the window."

"It's beautiful." She marveled.

"Do you know the first thing I thought of when I saw it?" he asked, his eyes meeting hers. She shook her head. "I thought that's the color of Harlow's eyes."

She blinked, looking down again at the stunning ring.

"I hadn't thought of you in so long, it was strange to think of you in that moment, but memories of you and me, the first time I met your eyes in that school hall and at the beginning of our relationship came flooding back to me. Each one, so precious to me as it was one of the few times in my life that I felt like I truly had purpose. To be your devoted boyfriend." He replied, tears welling up, making them glisten. "I walked right into that shop and bought it. I wanted it so I could feel that feeling every time I looked at it, and I have carried it with me as a reminder of you ever since."

Taking the ring, he slipped it on her ring finger, a perfect fit, and looked up at her waiting for an answer as he asked again, "Will you marry me, Harlow?"

Looking down at the ring and through her tears, she whispered her answer, "Yes." With unbridled joy, Rex rose, lifting her off her feet, swinging her around, both laughing through their tears of happiness. She wrapped her legs around his waist, and as their lips touched, it sealed the promise they had made today for their future.

One month later, Rex and Harlow stood together, his arms wrapped around her as they watched the second pink line appear on the home pregnancy test. He blinked, not believing his eyes, as she turned in his arms and uttered those words that he longed to hear, "You're going to be a daddy."

CHAPTER 13

Summer was in full swing. The end of school came and went, and Harlow and Ty moved into his condo. Living together came naturally, his space becoming theirs so easily, and Rex had never been happier. He watched as the summer days passed and Harlow's baby bump made an appearance. That beautiful swell, a symbol of his rebirth. This new life they were starting together.

One night as he watched her remove her robe after a shower, naked in front of him, he took in her bump and asked, "When do you want to get married?"

She turned, a nightshirt in her hands. "Anytime, honestly Rex, I don't need a big wedding. The first time I got married, it was this huge over the top thing. It never felt like my wedding, more like something his parents wanted." Rex nodded, taking in her words as she slipped the nightshirt over her body and crawled onto the bed, over him, to straddle his hips. "I just want something simple, our immediate families and closest friends. It doesn't need to be anywhere fancy, to be honest. A park, this apartment, I don't know. Even Meeting Grounds would suffice. All that matters to me is that I marry you and become your wife."

"I can't wait to call you Mrs. Johnson," he said, running his hands under her sleep shirt and up her bare back, relishing the silky-smooth skin under his fingertips as they settled on her hips.

She moaned, rubbing herself over his growing erection over his briefs. There was something he wanted to try before he made love to her tonight. "I want to taste you," he said, pulling her forward. "Climb over me and straddle my face."

"I've never done that." She said hesitantly, her face flushing with heat and self-consciousness.

"Then it will be a first for both of us," he replied. "Grip the headboard and grind yourself against me. I want to be buried in all that sweetness."

Hesitantly, she did as he asked, straddling his shoulders, spread wide, her bare heat over his face. He curled his arms around her thighs, pulling down as he licked her sensitive swollen folds. Taking her bundle of nerves between his lips, he sucked, and she gasped his name, white-knuckling the headboard as she cried out, her voice ragged and needy.

Her desire-filled cries spurred him on as he lapped at her softness, bringing her higher while, lost to sensation, she rocked unabashedly against his mouth. Feeling her legs tense, he brought her over the edge, the familiar gush of her arousal flooding his tongue with sweetness as he drank her in and softly brought her down until she merely trembled. She eased back onto his chest; her face flushed and eyes hazy with satisfaction as she glanced down at him, his chin wet with her climax. She slid off him and captured his mouth, tasting her musky arousal on his lips and tongue. It was the most erotic thing Rex had ever experienced as she pulled down his briefs freeing his member and straddled him, sinking onto his hard length and throwing her head back in ecstasy, her blonde hair like a golden halo in the lamplight of the room. He met her movements, savoring each undulation of her hips as she rose and fell on him, finding her pace and pleasure. *Is there anything more beautiful than this?* Taking her in with reverence, so lost in desire her eyes fluttered closed as she pulsed and rippled around him and let out a long-drawn-out moan, making him lose control and follow her. As they came down from the high, Harlow climbed off him and curled around his body, resting her head on his chest, both in a bubble of lust and immeasurable love. His hand came over her belly, and he looked up at her, their eyes meeting with contentment as he caressed the soft swell. Just as he did, he felt the tiniest thump against his palm. His eyes darted to hers as he asked excitedly, "Did you feel that?"

"I did!" she squealed, both stilling to see if it would happen again. Nothing. Harlow frowned and leaned in, kissing Rex sweetly. Pulling back, she settled on his chest, her hand on her belly as he held her, and she sighed. "I am so happy."

He pulled her tighter to him, those four words meaning so much more to him than she realized. There was a time not so long ago, he doubted he could make her happy. Still lost in a state of self loathing he was sure he would never find happiness, let alone bring happiness to someone else. And here they were, on the edge of their forever, a baby on the way, lives merging, and there were just two more things left to do. Adopt Ty and marry her. The first would have to be done after they were married, but now was the time to focus on a wedding. He had taken heed of her earlier words, requesting something simple, and knew exactly who to recruit to help him. As a plan formulated in his mind, he kissed her head, hearing her breath steady as she fell asleep in his arms. He lay there, Harlow curled around him as he planned their perfect wedding and how to surprise her with it.

* * *

REX DROVE onto the yard of Rami and Savanah's house and saw them on the front yard, kicking a large bouncy ball with an almost two-year-old Micah, and Savanah was curled up on a blanket with their six-month-old daughter, Presley. The weather was a beautiful late September day, and their yard was full of colorful leaves from the oak and maple trees sheltering the front yard.

He got out of his Jeep, little Micah running towards him, his curly brown hair shimmering in the sun. "Hey there," he said, scooping him into his arms and lifting him high in the sky. Micah stretched his arms and legs out, as if becoming an airplane, and Rex flew him around before planting a kiss on his head, resting him on his hip and walking over to Rami and Savanah.

"Hey, man!" Rami greeted. "What brings you here today?"

"How's Ty and Harlow?" Savanah asked curiously, picking up little Presley and hoisting her onto her hip. "Juli, Emersyn, and I dropped by Meeting Grounds the other day, and her baby bump has popped out. She's so cute," Savanah gushed.

Rex smiled; Harlow was now 22 weeks along and looked adorable with her t-shirts stretching over her growing belly. "They are both great, and I'm actually here to see if I can recruit your help. I was wondering, Savanah, if you could pull off a surprise wedding?"

"For you and Harlow, heck yeah, I can?" she said excitedly. "What do you have in mind?"

"In two weeks, Thanksgiving weekend," he said. "I was thinking of the Sunday at Meeting Grounds. Something simple, just closest friends and family. Followed by a Thanksgiving feast to celebrate all that we have to be thankful for."

"I love that idea so much!" she said eagerly. "I can already see the setup for the ceremony in the back room. We can use the seating already there, and it will be eclectic and cool. Oh, Rex, this is a brilliant idea."

"Can I leave it with you? I want this to be a complete surprise for Harlow until the day of, so you work your magic and do what you need to do to make it happen."

"On it!" she said, handing little Presley over to Rami. "I'm going to get started right away," she said, then walked towards the house and disappeared through the screen door.

Rami looked at Rex, his smile wide and eyes sparkling

as he said, "Well, it's about damn time you had your happily ever after."

* * *

HARLOW RELAXED ON THE SOFA; Rex had taken Ty out earlier that morning to do "guy things," so she was told. With her feet up, she flipped through a bridal magazine and relished the quiet. She had dogeared a few photos, but honestly nothing really jumped out at her. She had already had all the pomp and circumstance of a large wedding, and all she really wanted was for her and Rex to officially be married. She felt a flutter in her belly and put her hand over the swell, feeling another little push on her hand.

"Why hello there, little one." She said. "You agree with me, right? We don't need to have anything fancy." She said, setting down the magazine and putting both of her hands on her belly, feeling the sweet flutters and kicks. "I knew you agreed with me!"

An unexpected knock sounded at the door, startling her, and she walked over, peeking through the peephole to see Juli, Emersyn, and Savanah. She pulled her t-shirt over her belly and took a quick glance at her appearance in the entrance mirror, tucking the loose strands of her messy ponytail behind her ears as she opened the door.

"What are you all doing here?" She asked, glancing between them, and noticing the garment bags slung across Savanah and Emersyn's arms and the huge makeup case in Juli's hand. Her eyes darted between them again as she asked, "What's all this about?"

"We're your glam squad." Juli announced as she walked inside, putting the case on the kitchen island and pulling out her phone, pointing at her to take a video. "Surprise! Today is your wedding day!"

"What?" Harlow asked, not sure she had heard her correctly. "I thought I heard you say wedding day."

"You heard correctly." Savanah said, holding up the garment bag she was holding and unzipping it to take out a gorgeous long - sleeved, high-collar vintage gown, with a delicate lace high-waisted bodice and pleated skirt that flowed to the ground. It was a rich antique ivory, and instantly Harlow was in love.

"It's the most beautiful dress I have ever seen." She said, touching the intricate lace and smiling at her friends. "Did you plan this?"

"All Rex's idea. We were just recruited to help." Emersyn said, putting her hand on Harlow's shoulder.

Harlow could feel the tears prick her eyes before they hit her cheeks as she started to laugh between her tears, and she exclaimed, "God, I love him!"

"We have two hours before the wedding, so we need to get to work!" Juli exclaimed. "We can't be late, as Rex and Ty will be waiting."

"Where?" Harlow asked as they led her towards the bedroom.

"That secret we're not divulging, so don't ask!" Savanah giggled, the other ladies mirroring her.

The next hour was a blur of makeup brushes, curling irons and bobby pins between happy tears. With her makeup and hair done, they helped her step into the dress, and she gasped, holding her hand to her mouth as tears threatened to escape again. The dress was a perfect fit, and everything she never knew she wanted.

Juli came up behind her, her hands on her shoulders as she looked at her reflection and said, "You, my dear friend, are stunning."

She turned, wrapping all three of her closest friends in a hug, and turned again to the mirror, taking in her reflection.

"You are just missing one last thing." Savanah said as she reached into a bag she brought with her, and produced a gorgeous crown of flowers in rich orange, yellow and cream. She set it on her head, her blonde locks framing the flowers like a halo. As she took in her reflection, that of a blushing bride on her wedding day, Harlow was certain all her dreams were about to come true.

* * *

"STOP PACING." Steve ordered Rex with a laugh. "Em just messaged me that they are on the way."

Their small group of guests were filing in, everyone taking their seats. Rex's family on one side, and Harlow's on the other. Holly and the staff of Meeting Grounds were there. Jeremy and his girlfriend, Carrie, along with all the parents of Prairie Sound, holding babies and toddlers and keeping the chaos at bay. Rex was dressed in a sharp black suit, with a burnt orange tie and Rami, Layne and Steve all wore similar suits, with yellow ties, and all had corsages of wheat and fall foliage pinned to their lapels. They stood at the front of a makeshift aisle, as Savanah's van pulled up to the front of Meeting Grounds and Holly jumped up to slowly close the sliding door of the backroom giving everyone a knowing wink. Rami reached for his acoustic guitar and started to play. Rex listened carefully, immediately recognizing the song. "I Remember You", by Skid Row, a song that reminded him of where they came from. *Perfect.*

Then the barn door slid open, grandmothers directing Tabitha and Tyson down the aisle as Ty held a wooden box with the rings and Tabitha spread leaves down the aisle with a flourish. Tabitha gave Rex a toothy grin, and Tyson looked so completely enchanted by the pretty little girl in her fluffy orange dress beside him, he almost tripped over his feet and dropped the ring box. Rex could hear the little chuckle from Layne as he whispered, "And so it begins."

Emersyn and Savanah followed, taking their spots opposite the men, in their lace cocktail dresses in different fall hues. Juli came next, obviously the maid of honor and Harlow's official best friend. Her dress was a little longer and was a rich gold color. Rex smiled at the ladies as everyone rose to their feet and he stepped forward, seeing past the guests to where his angel stood. And that was exactly what she looked like, an angel. The woman who, despite all doubt, gave him a chance to prove himself. The woman who stood by him patiently, put her trust in him and allowed him to do what he needed to do to be the best he could be for her and her son. She gave him a second chance, a chance at redemption, and now she was here, before him, ready to become his wife. She walked slowly down the aisle, walking alone, a strong independent woman who had walked alone for so long but would be walking beside him for the rest of their lives. Harlow reached the end of the aisle, the unshed tears so close to escaping, but she swallowed down to try to temper her emotions. He blinked away his own tears, for the first time not feeling the searing burn of pain and regret constricting his chest. His tears today were those of a man that was looking at his forever, here before him in a beautiful dress. Harlow took his hand as they turned to each other and the marriage commissioner stepped forward.

"Welcome, everyone!" he said. "I've been directed to make this short and sweet as I understand Rex and Harlow have waited a long time for this day and don't want to delay it any further so with that, Harlow, let's start with your vows."

"Well, I didn't exactly have a chance to write anything down..." she began with a roll of her eyes, making everyone laugh. "...but I think I can wing it." She looked down at their joined hands and let out a long exhale, her gorgeous blue eyes drifting back to his. "I was 15 when I met you, and the first thing I noticed was your blue mohawk was the same color as your eyes and I thought, well hey that's cool." she said, everyone snickering with her words. "I also noticed your charisma. You were like a bright light in the darkness, drawing people in with your crass mouth and own brand of charm. I was a girl smitten, and those were some pretty crazy times," said with a wiggle of her eyebrows. Rex smiled and nodded. "Then, I saw you here again, 12 years later, older, mohawk gone, a man not hiding who he had become and still battling the ghosts of his choices. Seeing you again felt like fate in a way. Like how in all the coffee shops in St. Augustine, you ended up walking into mine. I think fate has always played a part in our story. Guiding us down paths that may have broken most people, but only revealed our strengths. Fate brought us back together at the right place and at the right time for both of us to complete the journey together. I am so grateful to fate right now. I am so grateful that it brought me back to you, and I am so excited to continue the rest of this journey called life together. I love you, Rex Johnson, always have, always will."

Rex blinked, tears started to trail down his cheek, and she reached up and wiped them as he swallowed down the emotion and took a few deep cleansing breaths so he could talk. "Well, if that is winging it, I am royally screwed here." he laughed, the guests joining in. He looked to the ceiling, willing himself to stop crying so he could speak.

"It's okay, baby, tell me what's on your heart." She whispered.

His gaze met hers and his heart filled with the most profound gratitude he had ever felt in his life. This woman had brought him back from the dead and reminded him that there was so much more life to live. *What can I say to express what this means to me?* Pulling himself together, he gazed into the eyes of his one and only love and said simply, "I wish I had this big, long speech telling you about all the ways I love you, but the truth is I could be here for days, listing them off and it still wouldn't be enough time. Simply, you, Harlow, are the love of my life. I love you more than anyone or anything in this world. Correct that, I love you, Ty and our baby..."

he said, putting his hands on her bump. "...more than anything in this world. And I cannot wait to spend the rest of my life with you and our little family."

Harlow beamed at him as she said, "That was so perfect!"

The marriage commissioner stepped forward and asked, "Rings?"

Harlow's mother gestured to Ty, who stepped forward carrying the little wooden box. Rex crouched down and gave him a wink as he took out the simple gold bands and handed them to the Commissioner. He held them up, saying, "Rings are a symbol of unending love. When you wear them, be reminded of your commitment here today." He handed one band to Harlow, and she took Rex's hand as she repeated after the commissioner, "I Harlow, marry you, Rex. I come today to give you my love, to give you my heart and my hope for our future. I promise to bring you joy, to be your sanctuary when you are lost and to love you more each day." With that, she slid the ring on his finger.

The Commissioner handed Rex a ring and asked him to repeat after him, "I, Rex, marry you, Harlow. I come today to give you my love, to give you my heart and my hope for our future. I promise to bring you joy, to be your sanctuary when you are lost and to love you more each day." His eyes locked on hers he slid the ring on her finger and took her hands.

"Then by the power vested in me by the Province of Manitoba, I now pronounce you husband and wife. Rex, you may now kiss your bride!"

Without a moment's hesitation, Rex took her face in

his hands, looked deep into her loving eyes and lowered his lips to kiss her deeply. The guests cheered, whooped, and hollered as they rose to their feet, clapping, and Harlow smiled against his lips as she breathed out, "my forever."

EPILOGUE

20 YEARS LATER

Rex peered out of Ty's bedroom window looking down at the guests forming in the yard and smiled taking in his bandmates, Rami and Steve with their salt and pepper hair and Savanah, now her natural blonde with silver highlights, yet looking as young as the day they met her. Emersyn, who looked like she hadn't aged a day, had her arm around Steve, looking up at him still with the same love and devotion as the day they were married. He remembered that wedding like it was yesterday; he was just at the beginning of his sobriety back then. Rex smiled at the memory, 24 years sober, internally beaming with pride as he heard Harlow come into the room, sniffling a handkerchief dabbing at her eyes. He turned and let out a laugh as he put his arms out to his weeping wife. "Honey, stop crying; you're going to embarrass the kid."

"Yeah, Mom! Are you going to blubber like that all the way down the aisle?" Ty asked, straightening out his tie and catching their gazes in the full-length mirror. He turned, his floppy blonde hair going into his eyes, and said, "Do I look okay?"

"You look amazing, Son," Rex said, putting his hand on his shoulder. Ty gave them both a grateful look and put his arms out for a hug. Both stepped in, their son towering over them. "We are so proud of the man you have become."

Ty glanced at Rex and smiled. "It's because of the example you gave me, Dad."

His heartfelt words made Rex's emotions rise in his chest, and he cleared his throat, willing himself not to cry like Harlow was.

"Are you ready?" Harlow asked, gazing up at her one and only son.

"Yes!" he replied with surety as they walked out of his childhood bedroom and made their way down the stairs to the main floor of the house. In the kitchen, Micah and Sebastien stood, looking dapper in their tailored suits as Ty approached them. Rex looked at the two boys, now both in their early twenties and musicians themselves.

When Rami told him that Micah had started a garage band with Sebastien, Rex just laughed, all the memories of those days playing in Layne's dingy garage, dreaming about sharing their music with the world and making their dreams of stardom come true coming back to him. After over 35 years of performing together and Prairie Sound was still gigging with their greatest hits, with rumblings of a lifetime achievement award on the horizon. *How time flies.*

The processional music started breaking Rex from his thoughts, and Ty leaned down for Harlow to give him one last kiss before Rex and Harlow walked out the patio door and down the aisle hand in hand. She glanced up at him and gave him a look he knew so well, asking him with her eyes, *do you remember the last time we walked down an aisle?*

He squeezed her hand in acknowledgment, and she smiled, both remembering their perfect impromptu wedding day 20 years ago. Four months after their amazing wedding, Harlow gave birth to their first daughter, Scarlett, and two years later, her sister Quinn arrived, followed in quick succession by Ivy 15 months after that. With them now being a family of six, they considered trying one more time for another boy, but honestly once they had Ivy their family felt complete. Besides, Ty was all the son Rex needed. He had quickly adopted him after they were married, and his last name was changed to Johnson. Although logically he knew they weren't blood, from the day he looked into his blue eyes, his face chocolate smeared from his stolen cookie, Rex knew Ty was destined to be his son. Besides being a terrific son, Ty was the epitome of an awesome big brother and kept a close eye on his gaggle of sisters like a protective big brother should. He was kind and doting on them, and Harlow would always comment that he would one day be an amazing husband. Now here he was, their only son, about to marry the love of his life.

Rex and Harlow took a seat next to their girls in the front row as Sebastien with Presley followed by Micah with Belle came down the aisle. Ty followed, striding confidently, his tall lanky frame sure and quick as he slapped hands and bumped fists as he went down the aisle. That was their son. Bold and confident and so different from the soft-spoken, shy boy he was when Rex met him. Once Ty found his voice, there was nothing stopping him. He was funny, outgoing and so damn smart, it blew Rex's mind. His passion for dinosaurs having turned to a passion for fossils in his teens, he had just graduated with a Master of Science degree and was now a Taphonomist, or a fancy way to say he was a scientist that studied the fossilization process. When he told them he wanted to study fossils, they never thought he could make a career out of it, but somehow, he managed to find his way and was now successfully doing what he loved.

Ty took his place as everyone rose and a harpist played. Rex glanced across the aisle to Juli, her hand full of tissues as she dabbed her doe-like eyes and stared down the aisle at Layne and their beautiful daughter, Tabitha.

Rex glanced back at his son, his ocean blue eyes wide and brimming with tears, as Tabitha Stark, dressed in an over-the-top princess gown that made her look like she floated instead of walked, came down the aisle towards him. As Layne passed them, he gave Rex a knowing smirk, which made him chuckle. Layne was almost completely grey now, and had subtle lines appearing on his face, indicating a life well lived. They stood before the minister as he asked, "Who gives this woman to this man?" Layne, his chin high and proud, said, "Her mother and I do." before he placed Tabitha's hand in Ty's and returned to Juli, who was full out crying now, and he pulled her to his side, rubbing her back.

Throughout the ceremony, Rex watched as his son

committed his life to the woman he had loved since they were children, and somehow this moment felt full circle. Harlow nestled into him, glancing up to meet his gaze. *God, I love her.* This life they had created was so vibrant and rich, and now, seeing their son cross over to his forever, Rex couldn't help but think that perhaps there was a greater power at play here.

With the ceremony over, the party was in full swing. The huge tent that had been erected on the side yard of their property, just outside St. Augustine, was full of loud music and laughter. Rex glanced at the house proudly, remembering the day they had moved in. They had purchased this land and built this house just after Scarlett was born, realizing they were going to need more space if they wanted to grow their family. The two story, modern home they built was designed to fit both their needs and lifestyle, and he loved their quiet country property.

Layne sauntered over and clapped Rex on the back, two glass bottles of Coca-Cola in his hand. He handed one bottle to Rex, and the men clinked them in a toast. "To Ty and Tabitha, may they have a happy life and give us lots of grandbabies." Layne said, making them both chuckle.

"Did we miss a toast?" Rami asked, walking up with Steve at his side. Both men held bottles of Coke too and clinked with Layne and Rex.

"We were just toasting to grandchildren," Rex answered.

A low rumble of laughter came from Steve's throat, and he shook his head. "Can you guys believe we're standing here, wondering which of us is going to be a grandfather first? When did we get so old?"

The men all laughed and glanced over to where Micah was dancing with Belle, their eyes locked on each other with intensity, and to Sebastien, who was swinging around Presley on the dance floor, making her giggle. They all looked at each other, their gazes meeting. "I think the better question is, whose kids are getting married next?" Rami asked.

Rex mused about that a moment and glanced over to Ty and Tabitha stealing kisses on the dance floor as he replied, "I think we have a lot of amazing things to look forward to in the future, my brothers."

Through all of life's challenges and triumphs, these four men had stood together as bandmates, best friends, and brothers. And as they stood side by side now, contentedly watching the women they loved and their beautiful families celebrate these abundant lives they had created, they clinked their bottles again, wide smiles on their faces, knowing that their journey together was far from over.

ALSO BY TANYA RENEE

Primrose Series

Prairie Sky

Prairie Nights

Prairie Fire

Prairie Hearts

Prairie Sound

Prairie Rain

Prairie Prestige

Prairie Roads

With The Band

Finding Direction

Love Notes

On The Edge Of Forever

MORE FROM SERENADE PUBLISHING

Songbird

By Sarah Williams

Brigadier Station Series

By Sarah Williams:

The Brothers of Brigadier Station

The Sky over Brigadier Station

The Legacies of Brigadier Station

Christmas at Brigadier Station

Heart of the Hinterland Series

By Sarah Williams:

The Dairy Farmer's Daughter

Their Perfect Blend

Beyond the Barre

The Outback Governess (A Sweet Outback Novella)

The Spring of Love Series

By Virginia Taylor

Forever Delighted

Forever Amused

Forever Heartfelt

The Tooth Fairy Chronicles

By Victoria Rocus

Tooth Decay With A Side Of Fae

Toothaches And Wedding Cakes

Baby Tooth And Tangled Roots

Wisdom Tooth And The Awful Truth

Missing Teeth And What Lies Beneath

Toothless Grins And His Father's Sins

For more information visit:

www.serenadepublishing.com

ACKNOWLEDGMENTS

First, I want to thank my readers for your loyalty and love. Without your readership I wouldn't have been able to live my dream. You inspire me to write more, dream bigger and give me much needed validation when I need it most. Thank you for being awesome.

As always, I want to acknowledge Sarah Williams, CEO of Serenade Publishing and fellow romance author who continues to be incredible to work with. As a new author you don't know what to expect from a publisher and you've created such a nurturing community for authors that both informs and inspires. Your dedication and hard work you put into my works as well as the other authors of Serenade, does not go unnoticed. Thank you.

To my husband Bart who listens to all my story ideas even if means pausing his TV shows or putting down his book. You are my constant and biggest support. I love you endlessly.

To my kids, Theo and Raina, two of the coolest human beings I know. The way you see and tackle life inspires me every day. I love being your mom!

And lastly, I simply want to say that writing this series started out as a self-indulgent way to share my love of music and turned into one of the most satisfying creative experiences of my life. Rex's story especially, is a reminder that no matter what trials you have been through, it is possible to reclaim your life. I'm very proud of the beautifully flawed characters in this series and hope their stories find a place in your heart, because they will forever have a special place in mine.

www.ingramcontent.com/pod-product-compliance
Lightning Source LLC
Chambersburg PA
CBHW060601190726
48283CB00003B/1110